"I

He sank his fingers deep into the silk of her hair, searching for the warmth of her scalp beneath, and tilted her head way back so he could have complete access to her mouth, which he took with deep, thrusting sweeps of his tongue. A remote corner of his brain was aware that his urgency was making him a little rough, and maybe he should ease up and let the poor woman catch her breath, but there was no time for that now. He'd waited too long and there were too many possible ways for their lips to fit together, tasting and nibbling, stroking and tugging, and the taste of her—a delicious combination of white wine and buttery icing from the cake—was far too delicious for him to slow down.

More. He needed more.

"I want you." Jesus, was that him with that guttural and animalistic voice that sounded as though it belonged to a caveman? Too far gone to manage gentle, he grabbed fistfuls of her hair, learning the feel of it, and then ran his fingers over her forehead and dimpled cheeks, and across those lips that were slick and swollen now, but still smiling. "You have no idea how much I want you."

Books by Ann Christopher

Kimani Romance

Just About Sex
Sweeter Than Revenge
Tender Secrets
Road to Seduction
Campaign for Seduction
Redemption's Kiss
Seduced on the Red Carpet
Redemption's Touch
The Surgeon's Secret Baby

ANN CHRISTOPHER

is a full-time chauffeur for her two overscheduled children. She is also a wife, former lawyer and decent cook. In between trips to various sporting practices and games, Target and the grocery store, she likes to write the occasional romance novel. She lives in Cincinnati and spends her time with her family, which includes two spoiled rescue cats, Sadie and Savannah, and a rescue hound, Sheldon, who terrorizes the cats and patrols the perimeter for squirrels and deer. Her next Kimani Romance titles, *Sinful Temptation* (February 2012) and *Sinful Seduction* (March 2012), introduce Alessandro and Antonios Davies, the Twins of Sin.

If you'd like to recommend a great book, share a recipe for homemade cake of any kind, or if you have a tip for getting your children to stop bickering, Ann would love to hear from you through her website, www.AnnChristopher.com.

ANN
CHRISTOPHER

THE SURGEON'S SECRET BABY

KIMANI
ROMANCE

If you purchased this book without a cover you should be aware
that this book is stolen property. It was reported as "unsold and
destroyed" to the publisher, and neither the author nor the
publisher has received any payment for this "stripped book."

Special thanks and acknowledgment
are given to Ann Christopher for her contribution
to the Hopewell General miniseries.

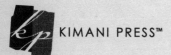

KIMANI PRESS™

PLEASE RECYCLE

THIS PRODUCT IS RECYCLABLE

Recycling programs
for this product may
not exist in your area.

ISBN-13: 978-0-373-86225-2

THE SURGEON'S SECRET BABY

Copyright © 2011 by Harlequin Books S.A.

All rights reserved. The reproduction, transmission or utilization
of this work in whole or in part in any form by any electronic, mechanical
or other means, now known or hereafter invented, including xerography,
photocopying and recording, or in any information storage or retrieval
system, is forbidden without written permission. For permission please contact
Kimani Press, 225 Duncan Mill Road, Toronto, Ontario M3B 3K9, Canada.

This is a work of fiction. Names, characters, places and incidents are
either the product of the author's imagination or are used fictitiously,
and any resemblance to actual persons, living or dead, business establishments,
events or locales is entirely coincidental.

® and TM are trademarks. Trademarks indicated with ® are registered in
the United States Patent and Trademark Office, the Canadian Trade Marks
Office and/or other countries.

www.kimanipress.com

Printed in U.S.A.

Dear Reader,

Here's what brilliant surgeon Thomas Bradshaw likes: working hard, playing hard and women. Here's what he doesn't like: surprises. Too bad he's about to get blindsided by the biggest surprises of his life.

First surprise? He has a kid. A precocious eight-year-old son who will die soon if he doesn't receive a kidney transplant, to be more specific.

Second surprise? The kid's mom, Lia Taylor, a woman so beautiful and intriguing that he has a hard time thinking straight when she's around.

Biggest surprise of all? This instant family may just be the best thing that's ever happened to him in his life....

Happy reading!

Ann

P.S. Don't forget to look for my next Kimani Romance titles, *Sinful Temptation* (February 2012) and *Sinful Seduction* (March 2012), which introduce Alessandro and Antonios Davies, the Twins of Sin.

To Richard

Special thanks to my wonderful editor, Kelli Martin, and to the other ladies in the Hopewell General series, Brenda Jackson, Maureen Smith and Jacquelin Thomas, for being so delightful to work with. Finally, big hugs and kisses to Mom, for helping me with my medical questions. Guess I owe you some gingersnaps, eh?

Chapter 1

Accusing gazes followed Special Agent Lia Taylor through Hopewell General Hospital.

They burned twin laser holes in the back of her head as she toured the facility, which was so massive, foreign and overwhelming to her that she might as well have been dropped via parachute into Beijing or Abu Dhabi. Her first-day jitters intensified, threatening to cause an ulcer in the lining of her churning stomach.

How in God's name had she, an FBI systems analyst with an impeccable record, landed herself here, in this hospital and this predicament? How could this possibly work? When would she ever go back to life as she knew it?

Soon? Never?

She felt like a tiny little fish, so far out of water that she'd never make her way back to her pond again. It didn't help that the immortal words of Judy Garland's Dorothy Gale kept running through her overwrought brain:

Toto, I've a feeling we're not in Kansas anymore.

No one in the building seemed to speak her language—she caught snippets of conversation from passing personnel, which included incomprehensible phrases like, *So, you're thinking bowel disimpaction? Dude. I hope you're ready to glove up and dig in*, and *Did you finally get rid of that GOMER?* and *Negative appendix? Now what?* She was sure she stuck out like a surgical clamp on a chest X-ray. Worse was the creeping certainty that people were staring and whispering as she passed, muttering darkly about the things she'd done and what she was:

Hacker.

Thief.

Criminal.

Or maybe those accusations were only in her mind.

Man, she hoped so.

Picking up the pace, which was tricky because of her pencil skirt and black pumps, she hurried after her new boss, Germaine Dudley, M.D., chief of staff. He seemed determined to lose her in this labyrinth, possibly because if she disappeared forever into the depths of, say, nuclear medicine, he'd never have to deal with her again.

They would not be winning any popularity contests with each other, she and the good doctor. Oh, no. And while she might be imagining the disapproving glances of everyone else around her, his were the real deal.

"This is the back way into the E.R." Dr. Dudley

reached out a weathered brown hand and smacked the wall switch plate, making the heavy metal doors whoosh open ahead of them. They strode into yet another nerve center—the hospital seemed to have dozens of them—where so many scrubs-and-Crocs-wearing people hustled by it was as though she'd stepped into Grand Central Station. "This is the easiest way to get here from the cafeteria, if you ever need to."

"Great."

He pointed. "The admissions desk is on the other side of that door. This is the nurses' station, of course."

"Of course," she murmured.

Without breaking stride, he shot her yet another narrow-eyed look over his shoulder, his lab coat flapping as though it, too, was irritated with her. "Am I boring you?"

"No," she said, and decided it was past time for her to grow a backbone where this man was concerned. He was not, after all, the Antichrist, even if he was in a position to make her life uncomfortable for a while, and they needed to get a few things straight. "But I can see you're not thrilled to be my tour guide, and I feel bad for taking you away from your real duties. Maybe someone else can show me the rest of the hospital…?"

The suggestion made him stop and snort with obvious disbelief. "Nice try, but I don't think it's a good idea for me to let you out of my sight. Do you? You might break into patient or employee records next. Why would you limit your hacking to the sperm-bank database?"

She'd earned that, yeah, but she didn't like hearing it said aloud, and she hated being under this pompous bastard's thumb. He may look something like Danny

Glover, but he had none of the actor's warmth or, as far as she was concerned, humanity.

Hitching up her chin, she got in his face. Screw it. What was the worst that could happen? Being fired? Hauled in by the police? Whatever it was, it was a sunny day in the park compared to what she was already facing in her personal life.

"If I'm so untrustworthy, Doctor, then why don't you throw me out and call the police? I hate to hang around where I'm not wanted. In fact, why don't I just go?"

For emphasis, she took a step toward the nearest glowing Exit sign, and that brought Dudley to heel, just like she'd known it would. Putting a hand on her arm, he stopped her and lowered his voice. "I don't think so. I don't like you, and I think you're a criminal who should be prosecuted to the fullest extent of the law, but this isn't about me. This is about what's best for Hopewell General, and the hospital—"

He caught himself with a grimace, but she already knew and took the opportunity to rub it in. Just a little.

"The hospital can't afford another scandal so soon, can it? Not after all that nasty publicity about your intern who was stealing narcotics from the hospital to support his habit." She tsked. "That was unfortunate, wasn't it?"

Dudley stilled, his face slowly hardening into stone. She waited.

"*Allegedly* stealing narcotics," he said finally, and she knew she'd won. This round, anyway.

"Right." Feeling cheerier by the second, she smiled. "*Allegedly.* Whatever. The bottom line is, I need you not to press charges, and you need me to build you a world-class security system to protect the hospital's computers. See? Win-win. So maybe we could work on not hating each other so much. What do you say?"

To her dismay, he continued to stare at her, but the vibe twisted and changed into something that made her skin crawl, especially when that slow gaze scraped down and over her body, as though he could see through her black suit to the parts of her body no man had seen in more years than she cared to count. Those brown eyes became thoughtful…considering…calculating. He was so obvious about it she could almost hear the clank of gears shifting in his devious little mind. It would have been funny except that she didn't have time for this kind of nonsense, not with—

No. She wouldn't think about that now. First things first.

"Maybe we could discuss this over dinner," he suggested, his voice as sleek and oily as a spill in the Gulf of Mexico.

"Hmm." She smiled sweetly, purely for the pleasure of seeing that flare of greedy lust in his expression right before she cut him off at the knees. "Just so you know, Doctor, I was the best shooter in my class at the academy, and I'm licensed to carry a concealed handgun with me wherever I go. Still want that dinner?"

His skin went pale around his frozen grin.

"Oh, well. Too bad. And please make sure to tell your wife that we've decided to keep our relationship on a professional level. I don't want her coming after me. Okay?"

Dudley goggled at her. "My wife?"

"Your *wife*." Lia jerked her head in the direction of a

woman behind the nurse's station. Though she quickly tossed her fall of sleek black hair, lowered her head and made a show of flipping through a patient chart, the woman had been tracking Lia's interaction with Dudley since the second they came into view. She was about thirty-five-ish, Lia guessed, and would have been stunningly beautiful if she hadn't been giving Lia the Medusa stare for the last several minutes. "She seems to be the jealous type."

Looking bewildered, Dudley turned to see whom Lia was referring to and spied the woman, who shot him a quick glare. His expression cleared with sudden understanding that made his face brighten to a stunning magenta. Lia considered the color change a dead giveaway to some sort of questionable behavior between him and Ms. Attitude, but Dudley apparently imagined himself to be quite the player and was now giving Lia the wide-eyed, innocent act. Lia played along, just for kicks. If this idiot wanted to delude himself into thinking that FBI agents couldn't read people's body language, then who was she to disabuse him of that notion?

"That's not your wife?" she asked.

"Ah, no," Dudley said, clearing his throat. "She's, ah, Kayla Tsang. Head of nursing in E.R.."

"She seems very interested in our conversation."

"I don't know what you're talking about." Keeping his resolute gaze straight ahead, Dudley resumed his march around the nurse's station. "And I need to get back to the office."

Lia ducked her head, careful to keep her smile to herself. "My mistake."

Yeah, it was time to get cracking, and, amusing as

the good doctor and his extracurricular activities were, they had nothing to do with Lia. Well, unless he tried to hit on Lia again; then she'd use what she suspected as leverage against him. But she didn't think it would come to that. Meanwhile, the sooner they got done with this ridiculous tour, the sooner she could get back to her new office and work on the security system, and the sooner she could return to the FBI after this leave of absence. They'd already wasted the better part of the morning.

"I'm just trying to understand what was going through your mind, Brown." A man's deep voice, low but hard-edged with annoyance, cut across the hubbub from the other side of the nurse's station. "Give me something to work with here."

Don't be nosy, Lia told herself, even though Dudley and everyone else, for that matter, were already glancing around and craning their necks like rubbernecking drivers on the highway. *It's none of your business.*

Her feet, unfortunately, didn't understand social niceties and were already slowing for a better look at the developing ass chewing. There was something compelling about that man's voice, something that caught her attention in a steel-jawed grip and didn't let go.

And then she saw him.

Not the red-faced and stammering Brown, a young guy—resident, she was guessing—who looked like a twelve-year-old who'd tried on his father's scrubs and was now horrified to actually be mistaken for a doctor.

No. Lia couldn't look away from the other guy. The angry one who had his back to her while he got in Brown's face.

About six feet tall, he, too, was dressed in scrubs—hell, everyone around here was—and had the broad-shouldered, narrow-waisted, round-assed combination of a born athlete or a gym rat. His gesturing arms were smoothly brown and sculpted, and he wore battered running shoes, which told her they saw action outside the corridors of this hospital. A stethoscope dangled around his neck at the base of his skull-trimmed head, and she hoped he wasn't about to whip it off and use it to strangle Brown, which seemed like a distinct possibility.

After several excruciating beats, the stammering and floundering Brown found his tongue and worked up an answer. "I didn't think—" he began.

Dr. Pissed Off snorted. "That much is clear."

"—that we needed a chest X-ray," Brown continued. "So I—"

"So you didn't order one." Dr. Pissed Off swelled with indignation, somehow taking up more than his fair share of the air and space around the nurse's station. "And now we've got a patient with a raging case of pneumonia, which should've been diagnosed yesterday. Does that about sum it up?"

Everyone within a twenty-foot radius was listening now. Oh, they kept up the pretense of working, sure, but the personnel behind the counter had their ears cocked as they tapped on their keyboards or spoke on the phone, and even the passing orderly and the patient he was wheeling on his gurney turned their heads to gape. Beside Lia, Dudley was watching with rapt attention, which, she figured, gave her permission to keep watching.

Brown had the good sense to keep his mouth shut. But if he'd hoped that would shorten his time in the dunce chair, he was sadly mistaken.

"I don't think you have the chops for this," said Dr. Pissed Off, whom she was beginning to think of as Dr. Jackass. "I really don't. Any third-year medical student would have ordered the film. Hell, anyone's who's ever watched half an episode of *Grey's Anatomy* would've ordered the film. I'm thinking you should've gone to law school, Brown."

Ouch. Low blow.

Brown seemed to think so too, because he jerked his chin up, grew a pair and tried to defend himself. "Look. I made a mistake. It won't happen again. I'm sorry."

Dr. Jerk was not impressed. "I don't want your apology," he said. "I want you to do your job. Now get out of here."

Brown wavered for a second, his humiliated and defiant gaze flickering between his tormentor and their avid audience. A couple of the nurses gave him an encouraging smile, which seemed to give him courage. He looked like he wanted to return to the battlefield and maybe fire off one last salvo, but he couldn't seem to find the guts.

Instead, he ducked his head and hurried off around the corner, heading for the elevators and, probably, a long day spent beating himself up for his honest mistake.

Poor guy. Lia's heart squeezed with sympathy as she watched him go. Was this kind of abuse dished out to the beleaguered residents on a daily basis? And did Dr. Pissed Off think he was God?

Dumb question. Yes, of course he did. Didn't all doctors?

"For God's sake," Dr. Evil muttered to no one, continuing his ridiculous little temper tantrum by slamming the patient's metal file on the counter as he strode off. Everyone jumped and then hastily resumed their busywork, as though they'd been so engrossed in minding their own business that they'd missed the whole interlude. "How am I supposed to teach these clowns?"

Something possessed Lia. She'd been accused, on more than one occasion, of being a crusader, and right now she felt the strong urge to find a cape and a sword and fly to the rescue of young Dr. Brown.

Idiotic, yeah, especially considering that she didn't know the guy, who could well be the worst student to ever claw his way through a sub-par medical school, but she couldn't just stand quietly by while his boss the jerk tore into him. Injustice of any kind, real or imagined, made her face burn with anger. And why was no one else standing up to the ogre and speaking out against his reign of terror?

"For God's sake." She kept her voice loud and clear as she spoke to Dr. Jackass's departing back. "How are residents supposed to learn when they're being bullied?"

A ringing silence bloomed like a nuclear explosion, giving her time to wonder if she'd gone too far.

And…yeeeeeaaah. She'd probably gone too far.

Jaws dropped. Heads swiveled in her direction. Wide-eyed looks were exchanged. Even Dudley raised his brows and gave her an are-you-crazy glance.

She waited with a growing sense of foreboding.

The bully paused, cocked his head as though he

wanted to make sure he'd heard right, and then wheeled around, facing her for the first time. His attention zeroed in on her, the big mouth, and she'd almost swear that everyone else ducked and scurried away so as not to be caught in the oncoming path of destruction. In that pregnant moment, she had a wild image of the indigenous people tying Ann Darrow to her sacrificial post and then sprinting back to the other side of that primitive gate, where it was safe from King Kong.

Only this was no King Kong. Not by a long shot.

Oh, man. The breath leaked out of her lungs in one quick whoosh, and she found herself caught in the fierce gaze from a pair of furious but extraordinary brown eyes. He had long lashes and straight brows that showcased a burning intensity and a keen intelligence. His dark skin was flushed. One edge of his full lips pulled back in a disbelieving sneer, which revealed a hint of both white teeth and a bracket of what would be dimples, if and when he ever smiled.

He was, in a word, stunning.

Shock hit Lia like the leather thong of a cracked whip.

In two long strides he was on her, right in her face. "*What* did you say to me?"

Locking her knees in place, Lia stood up to him because no one else had. "I said that if a student isn't learning, it's generally the teacher's fault."

A collective gasp, quickly stifled, rippled through the crowd of avid onlookers, all of whom were probably wishing they had an ICEE and a large buttered popcorn to go along with the show.

His eyes—his unforgettably amazing eyes—widened

with shock, probably because no one had challenged his arrogance in the last decade or so. Recovering quickly, he looked her up and down with cool disdain.

"Are you a licensed physician?"

"No," she admitted.

Triumph gleamed in his expression. "Then you don't know what the hell you're talking about, do you?"

With that, he gave Dudley a curt nod and strode off, sucking all the air out of the area with him. His departing back posed a real challenge to her. She wanted to hurl just the right comeback and prevent him from having the last word, but her mouth was dry and her brain was empty.

Best to just leave well enough alone. For now.

"In case you were interested," Dudley told Lia, flashing her an amused grin, "that was Dr. Bradshaw. The youngest ever head of surgery here and the best we've got."

Oh, she knew who he was, even though they'd never met. He bore a remarkable resemblance to someone very close to her, but now wasn't the time to get into personal details about her life. Soon, but not now.

"Hmm." Badly shaken and acutely aware of both her burning face and Dudley's curiosity, she tried to get her head back in the game. She'd confront the arrogant Dr. Thomas Bradshaw soon enough. Until then, she had a job to do and a role to play with her new boss. "Too bad no one ever taught him to be a kind human being."

"He's only kind on Tuesdays and Thursdays," said a new, male voice behind her. "So it looks like we're all out of luck today. Jerome Stubbs, RN. I just wanted to meet the woman who confronted the dragon in his lair. And you are…?"

Bracing for the worst—she was wrung out already, and her first day at this godforsaken hospital wasn't even halfway over yet—Lia turned to discover a grinning young man extending his hand to her. Relief hit her in a wave. Here, at last, was the friendly face of someone who didn't appear to be a jerk or have an agenda.

So she shook his hand, discovering that Jerome had a firm grip, which was another sign of trustworthiness as far as she was concerned.

"Lia Taylor. Computer security expert. Nice to meet you."

Jerome reached out and slung his arm around the shoulders of another man nearby, this one with dark skin and a mustache with goatee, scooping him into the conversation as well. "This is Dr. Lucien De Winter. Say hello to the dragon slayer, Lucien."

They all laughed, including Dudley, and Lia felt some of the seething tension of the last few minutes leach away from her.

"He's not so bad, you know," Lucien told her. "Thomas has standards that are exceptionally high. But he's not terrible once you get to know him. Bad, yeah, but not terrible."

"I'm not convinced," Lia said. "But you two seem perfectly nice. It's a pleasure to meet you."

"We know. We're a delight," Jerome assured her.

Still laughing, he headed back to the nurse's station. Lucien, meanwhile, waved his goodbye and disappeared into the cafeteria. Lia turned back to Dudley and discovered him watching her with a glimmer of amused respect in his eyes.

"What?"

Dudley grinned. "You're a piece of work. You should fit in just fine around here. If you don't commit any more felonies, that is."

Okay. She'd about had it with the male medical personnel around here.

"Don't we have a tour to finish?" she reminded him.

Dudley checked his watch and then held his arm wide, gesturing her toward the cafeteria. "We might as well get some coffee while we're here."

"Great," Lia agreed, but her troubled thoughts were already spinning in other directions.

Back to Thomas Bradshaw. Back to her son. Back to her dwindling options and growing desperation. Back to the twisty and uncertain path she'd chosen and would continue on until its end, whatever that end turned out to be.

She would walk this path, for Jalen.

Anything to save her son.

Chapter 2

"Hello, dearie." Thomas's receptionist looked up from her computer as he walked into the waiting area of his suite in the medical office building and shut the door against the dull roar outside. Sunny as usual, her blue eyes bright and her weathered, peaches-and-cream complexion flushed with the apparent thrill of another afternoon spent fielding patients for him, she slid her beaded bifocals down the bridge of her nose and gave him a critical once-over. "You haven't eaten lunch again, have you? Determined to wither away to the size of a tadpole, I suppose. Well, you can lead a horse to water, but you can't make the dumb bastard drink, can you?"

Thomas had to smile. "Good to see you, too, Mrs. Brennan." Though she'd been with him for the eight years since she stepped off the plane from Dublin to live with her daughter's family here in Alexandria, and he knew her first name full well—Aileen—he'd never dared use it. It seemed disrespectful somehow, and he was pretty sure she'd drop kick his ass into next week if he ever tried it. He, on the other hand, had to submit to *dearie, love, young Thomas* or whatever other silly nickname that she felt like bestowing on him. Not that he minded. Much. "How was your weekend? How's the grandbaby?"

"Oh, well, she's the little heart of my heart, now, isn't she? Working on one teeny little tooth in the front. Here's a picture."

She flipped around the digital frame on her desk, showing him a chubby and smiling green-eyed baby with yellow fuzz and a smear of what looked like spaghetti sauce across her face and, sure enough, the hint of a white tooth on her bottom gum.

Oh, man. What a beauty.

Staring at the child, he felt…a pang. Of…something.

Probably nothing more than hunger, not that he'd admit it to Eagle Eyes here.

"You're very lucky," he said.

"That I am." She spun the frame back into place and nailed him with that concern again. "And don't think that you've managed to distract me from your dietary habits, either, young man. Oh, is that coffee for me? Cream and two sugars?"

"Of course."

"Let's have it, then."

"I don't think so." He held the Starbucks cup just out of reach of her grasping hand, determined to get this bargain struck as soon as possible. "By accepting this beverage, you agree not to comment on my personal life. Deal?"

Mrs. Brennan glowered until her white brows ran straight across her forehead. "For how long?"

"The whole week."

"Go on, then," she said, snatching the cup out of his hand and drinking long and deep. "Nothing but trouble, you are. Here. Eat a protein bar. Get some nutrition."

She tossed him a bar from the inner depths of her desk drawer. God alone knew what all she kept in there; one of these times he meant to ask for a walleye fishing lure just to see if she could produce it.

He caught it with gratitude because he was still hungry, although he felt compelled to point out a pertinent fact. "I'll have you know I ate a turkey croissant on the elevator just now."

She didn't look remotely impressed. "A grown man like you? You ought to be ashamed of yourself calling that a meal. Eat the bar, and just say thanks."

Well, she had him there.

"Thanks. I'm going to see how many calls I can make before the meeting at one."

"Sign the letters on your desk for me."

"Aye-aye, Captain." He started down the hallway, ready to collapse into his chair and rest for a minute. Every one of his thirty-six years was really starting to show. Used to be he could stand and operate all day, see patients, handle meetings, go for a run, do paperwork into the wee hours and then collapse into the bed of his woman of the moment before getting up and doing it all again the next day.

Now all he wanted was a two-week nap.

And, come to think of it, a life.

"How were the residents this morning?" she called after him. "Giving you fits?"

Brown and his hapless stammering flashed through Thomas's mind, quickly followed by his beautiful defender. She'd been interesting, that one. There'd been something about her that almost distracted him from her unfortunate tendency to butt into the conversations of perfect strangers.

"Giving me fits?" His mind's eye focused in on the woman's smoky voice…the breasts that were plumped against the lacy white top she wore under that severe suit…the wide hips and shapely bare legs…the startling intensity in her brown eyes. His skin prickled with remembered awareness, and he could swear that the faint scent of her perfume, which was sophisticated and spicy, had followed him all morning. That was a neat trick, considering all the other, less pleasant smells the hospital had to offer. "You have no idea."

Inside his office, he collapsed into his chair, rested his elbows on the desk and his face in his hands. Man, he was tired. He'd been on last night, and then removed the diseased left lung of an unrepentant, forty-year smoker, which was the medical equivalent of redecorating the staterooms on the Titanic. Then he'd had rounds and the unfortunate run-in with Brown before he'd had a meeting with some of the other doctors in his practice group.

But that Brown thing…it bothered him.

Partially because the kid had been at the tail end of a thirty-hour stint, a point when it was hard for the best of them, even a perfectionist like himself, to fire on all cylinders. Partially because Brown was a competent physician and Thomas hadn't meant to let loose his temper and humiliate him like that. Partly because it dinged his ego to be read the riot act for his bad behavior by a stunning and undaunted woman, especially when he was at his most daunting.

Especially when he deserved it.

Who was she? Why was he still thinking about her?

He didn't know, but there was only one way to find out: he'd ask Dr. Dudley about her and track her down. Something was telling him he'd regret it for a good long time if he didn't.

His phone beeped, and Mrs. Brennan's voice came over the intercom. "Your da's on line one."

Brilliant. Just what he needed to make his day even more of a nonstop thrill fest.

And why did the woman insist on referring to his father as *Da* when she knew damn good and well that, as a retired admiral, the man would never appreciate or answer to anything as pedestrian and affectionate as *Da*, *Dad* or, God forbid, *Pops*.

He stared at the phone, wondering if he could pretend he hadn't heard.

"I know you heard me," Mrs. Brennan's voice said.

"Why would you think I'd want to talk to my father?"

"Don't be a twit, dearie. You can always talk to the man who gave life to you."

The man who gave life to him. That much was true, Thomas supposed, and the man had reared him—when he wasn't at sea, anyway—and instilled his relentless discipline in him. So, for that, Thomas was grateful.

On the other hand, they'd always had a prickly

relationship punctuated by periodic disownings, most notably when Thomas turned down his commission to the Naval Academy in favor of college and medical school, which were inferior enterprises as far as the Admiral was concerned.

Still. The man was the only blood he had since Mom died two years ago.

"Put him through," he said grudgingly, and the next thing he knew, the Admiral was booming over the speaker at him. The Admiral always boomed.

"I saw the full exposé in the paper this morning. All the details are finally coming out. Two-inch headline, Hopewell General Downplayed Drug Scandal—Fired Intern. Nice. What the hell kind of Mickey Mouse operation are you people running up there? And who's in charge of your PR? Donald Duck?"

"Thanks for calling." Thomas balanced the phone on his shoulder, found the stack of letters and started signing. "Nice of you to be concerned."

A snort from the Admiral. "Someone's got to be concerned. First the drug thing, then your buddy Lucien De Winter had to step down as chief resident because he was hooking up with one of his interns—"

Unbelievable. "They weren't hooking up," Thomas interjected. "They're engaged. As you well know."

As usual, the Admiral trampled right over Thomas's half of the conversation. "You folks are about to run a perfectly good hospital right into the ground with these scandals—"

"The hospital will recover."

"—and if you'd followed in my footsteps like you

were supposed to do, you wouldn't have these kinds of issues."

There it was. The inevitable reminder of the greatest of Thomas's alleged failings. His accomplishments, including his scholarships to Dartmouth and then Columbia for medical school and subsequent spectacular career as a surgeon, never made their way into these conversations.

"Good point," he said. "The military never has scandals."

"Don't you get snippy with me, boy," the Admiral began, but a commotion out in the reception area diverted Thomas's attention.

"I don't know who you think you are, missy." Mrs. Brennan's voice, outside his office and closing in now, sounded harassed and shrill, which was a disturbing first in all the years he'd known her. "But you cannot just march into Dr. Bradshaw's office and—"

"Watch me," said another woman's voice.

Wait a minute, Thomas thought, his heart rate kicking into overdrive as determined footsteps stopped outside his door. *I know that voice.*

And then, there she was, standing in his doorway.

Brown's defender, a woman who was, he now realized, as beautiful as any he'd ever seen.

Their gazes locked for a moment, during which she seemed to gather her thoughts and he seemed to forget how to breathe. Man, she was fine. Her cheeks were flushed with pretty color, and her eyes were a startling flash of brown fire. There was something about her body language—squared shoulders, fighting stance and firm chin—that told him she'd come armed for battle, and he discovered, much to his surprise, that he couldn't wait to engage her and see how well their wits matched up for round two.

"I need to talk to you," she told him. "It's important."

Something inside him answered even before he got his thoughts organized.

Yes. Everything between them felt like it could be important. Did she also feel it?

Slowly, he got to his feet.

"—and I don't know how you can practice medicine in that circus," the Admiral was now saying in his ear.

This was not the time for his father. "I'll call you back," Thomas said, and hung up on the Admiral's splutter of surprise.

Mrs. Brennan burst into the office, edging the woman aside and dividing her gaze, giving him an apologetic glance and the woman a killing glare. "I'm so sorry, Doctor. I don't know who on God's green earth this woman thinks she is."

This was not the time for Mrs. Brennan, either. "Give us a minute," Thomas told her.

Mrs. Brennan's jaw dropped. "But I can have security here in a jiff—"

"I'll call you if I need you."

Even Mrs. Brennan at her feistiest couldn't mistake the finality in his tone. "I hope you know what you're doing," she muttered darkly, slipping out the door.

The woman clicked the door shut behind her and crossed the room to stand in front of his desk. "Thank you. For your time."

Sudden urgency made his voice hard, but he needed to know.

"What's your name?" he demanded.

She hesitated. "Lia Taylor."

An unusual feeling of shame made him launch into his explanation even though he rarely, if ever, felt the need to make himself understood to others. Normally, he did his thing, which was performing his job to the best of his excellent ability, and if someone had an issue with his occasional abrasiveness, then that was just too damn bad. If people preferred a surgeon with a sweeter temper but unsteady hands, then that was their choice, right?

Normally, that was.

With Lia Taylor, on the other hand, he was happy to spill his guts.

Anything to convince her that he wasn't a complete SOB.

"Just so you know," he said, "Dr. Brown's earlier mistake means that our patient is unstable and needs antibiotics for several days. Which means that we have to postpone her surgery for several days. Which isn't good."

"Oh." Lia blinked. Something in her expression softened, and he felt a corresponding easing of his own tension. Did he have a chance with her, then, if she realized he wasn't a bastard? "It was none of my business."

"No, it wasn't."

"I'm not sure what got into me. I'm a crusader, I guess. I usually root for the underdog."

"Good to know. I'll bear that in mind."

"But that's not why I'm here."

"No?" His belly tightened with delicious anticipation. "Why are you here?"

It took several long beats for her to answer.

"I'm here about my son." She drew a deep breath, then another, clearly gathering courage to tell him something big. "I'm here about…our son."

Chapter 3

Our son.

The two words hung in the air, hovering over his head like one of those giant anvils that Road Runner was always using to nail Wile E. Coyote in those old Looney Tunes cartoons.

And then they hit him, along with the stinging realization that this woman had no personal interest in him whatsoever.

"Our son?" he echoed, reeling.

"Yes."

"Bullshit."

She seemed to have expected this reaction, because she flinched but quickly recovered, plowing ahead with grim determination. "I know you don't believe me, but he's sick. And I need your help."

Oh, okay. He got it. With a bitter laugh, he strode

to the door and opened it, the better to speed this little liar on her way. "Nice try. I hate to tell you this, but your theatrics won't get you to the front of my waiting list for new patients, okay? You need to wait your turn like everyone else. Now, if you'll excuse me—"

To his utter shock, she put her warm little hand on top of his where it rested on the knob, and stared up at him with such a wild mix of hope and desperation in her face that he had to turn away from it. "I'm not making this up. Look at me. I swear on Jalen's life that I'm not making this up. Please hear me out."

Jalen.

Weaker and more foolish than he needed to be where this one woman was concerned, he looked at her.

Mistake.

Tears sparkled in those big brown eyes, clinging to her black lashes and threatening to spill onto smooth brown cheeks that had to be the softest things in the world, not that he'd ever know. Worse was her unblinking earnestness, which was unexpected but unmistakable. Whatever else she might be, Lia Taylor didn't appear to be off her meds, a wacko or a plain vanilla liar.

Or maybe that was just his lust talking.

Snatching his hand free—maybe he could think better when she wasn't touching him—he stalked back to his desk, anxious to put some distance between him and her and between him and his growing sense of unease.

"Start talking," he said. "Why don't you start with explaining this miraculous event, since you and I have never laid eyes on each other before today, much less had sex." He let his gaze scrape down her body, lingering on a few key points, trying to insult her the way she'd insulted his intelligence by expecting him to believe this fairy tale. "You didn't think I'd forget having sex with you, did you, sweetheart? Because there's no chance of that. Let me assure you."

"Don't call me sweetheart. This is hard enough without you being patronizing." She shut the door again and took a few steps farther into the office. "And of course it wasn't an immaculate conception—"

He leaned against his desk, crossing his arms and his legs. "Oh, I get it. This is the part of the conversation where you try to convince me that we had sex after some college frat party and I was too drunk to remember."

"No, actually," she said, her voice cooling several degrees and her tears long gone by now, "I've never been sexually attracted to drunk people."

So she wasn't going to pursue that line of argument, eh?

Smart choice. Especially since the chance of him forgetting a night with her, drunk or not, were the same as him playing starting center for the L.A. Lakers. Anyway, he'd been too busy studying to have many drunk nights in college, and too careful of his future to have unprotected sex with random women.

"Well, feel free to enlighten me."

"My husband and I—" she began.

The H-word didn't sit well with him, which was insane. "You're married?"

"Widowed." She had the nerve to raise one delicate

brow with obvious annoyance. "Are you going to let me get a complete sentence out?"

He waved a hand for her to continue.

After a pause to make sure he wouldn't interrupt again, she started over.

"My husband was older than me. We wanted kids. He couldn't have them. So we went to a sperm bank." She hesitated. His belly knotted, apparently realizing before the rest of him that a missile strike was headed straight for the space between his eyes. "The Hopewell General sperm bank."

Thomas's heart stopped cold.

Lia's voice gentled, as though she knew that she was flipping his world up on its end. "I was artificially inseminated. I got pregnant. We were ecstatic." Tears sparkled in her eyes again, and she struggled, her voice cracking. "Until he was killed in a car crash before Jalen was born."

Ah, shit.

He waited, giving her time to collect herself, which was probably a mistake.

After a deep breath, she got it together enough to keep on kicking the ground out from under Thomas's feet. "That was nine years ago. Now Jalen is sick and he needs your help, which is why I'm here. The end."

It was the end, all right. The end of Thomas's ability to stand upright with his knees nice and strong. Bracing his palms on his desk for support, he took his time lowering himself into his chair and wished he could handle this crisis as well as he handled the ones inside the operating room.

Think, man. THINK.

Didn't Hopewell General have privacy policies in place to protect the anonymity of anonymous sperm donors?

Hell, yes.

He looked up to find her hovering over the desk, watching him intently, as though the world—their world—hung in the balance. Which, he supposed, it did.

"How do you know?" he wondered. "How do you know I'm the father?"

Her gaze wavered. "I…hacked into the hospital's records."

The words rattled around inside his head, making no sense. He tried to imagine what had to be involved in such a task—break-ins, firewalls, passwords, encryptions, decryptions and probably a whole bunch of other computer wizardry that he'd never heard of and could never understand.

"You…*hacked* into the records?"

"Yes," she said, defiant now. "I'd do anything for my son."

"You don't just hack into—"

"You do if you're an FBI analyst. And I hope you realize that I've just given you enough information to ruin my career and send me to jail for a long time. So I hope you'll use it wisely."

He was a bright guy, but it took his spinning thoughts way longer than it should have to coalesce into something coherent. "Hang on. *You're* the hacker?"

Impatience leached into her voice. *"Yes."*

"So what the hell were you doing with the chief of staff earlier, hanging out like you're new BFFs?"

"They don't want to put the hospital through the scandal of prosecuting me, so they've hired me to build a stronger security system."

"Jesus," he muttered.

Her lips twisted a little, as though she, too, appreciated the irony.

They watched each other for a couple of beats, both wary.

"Do you believe me now?" she asked.

His answer took much longer than it should have. An automatic and emphatic *Hell, no!* should have been flying out of his mouth, but it seemed stuck in his throat. Crazy, right? He hadn't signed up for a kid, had always taken steps to prevent producing a kid and wasn't ready for a kid. Hell, maybe there really wasn't a kid.

Maybe this complete stranger was looking for a baby daddy with resources to pay for the kid's braces. Maybe she'd researched him and his family and knew the kind of money they had. Maybe she wanted to get rich quick on child support. Other women had certainly tried, unsuccessfully, to tap into his wallet over the years, so he wouldn't be surprised. Plus, the hospital was up to its neck in scandals, and it wouldn't do his personal reputation around here any good if he turned out to have a baby mama, not that he'd ever cared too much about people's opinions of him, even his colleagues'.

And yet...

Hold up. There was no *and yet*, even if the idea of having a son tugged at some primal daddy thing inside him. He was too shrewd to be played for a fool.

"Why would I believe the word of an admitted hacker

and felon who barges into my office to tell me I have a son but doesn't have any proof? Or *do* you have proof? My bad."

Flashing him a look withering enough to melt his spine, she reached into a skirt pocket, pulled out a smart phone, tapped a couple of buttons and handed it to him without a word.

Whereupon his limbs froze with sudden paralysis.

If he looked at that picture, there was a chance that his life would change forever. Except that, looking into Lia's eyes, he couldn't shake the feeling that they'd passed that point of no return a while back.

Taking the phone, he looked.

"Oh, my God." His fingers tightened in a convulsive grip. "Oh, my God."

The kid—Jalen; his son's name was Jalen—was holding a disgruntled gray rabbit in his arms and smiling with delight into the camera. It would have been tempting to accuse Lia of somehow stealing a photo of Thomas when he was a child, but he'd never had a gray rabbit and certainly had never owned an *Avatar: The Movie* T-shirt.

The eeriness of it made his scalp tingle and the hair stand up on his arms.

He was looking into a younger version of his own face. The Mini-Me to his Dr. Evil. They could have been twins, separated by twenty-eight years.

They had the same chocolate skin with red undertones. The same point at the corner of their right ears. The same straight nose.

The boy's eyes were keen and intelligent and…

Oh, man. Those were his eyes, looking back at him.

Hell, they even had the same right eyebrow, which was flatter than the left.

He stared, looking for differences, and there were some, but not enough. Jalen had his mother's dimples and her high cheekbones, but he was, God help him, clearly Thomas's son. And suddenly, he couldn't look at the picture for one more second. Not one.

Too stunned to think, he handed the phone back to Lia, who gave him a moment by walking over to the window.

He stared down at his desk through the sudden blur of hot tears, and he couldn't decide if he was mostly stunned, mostly angry or mostly…

Thrilled.

He was a father. Jalen was his son.

"I'll want to meet him," he told her. "After the DNA tests."

He waited for some sort of refusal or outrage, but there was none.

"Okay," she said.

Good. She was savvy enough to know that the legalities had to be observed in cases like this. He liked that.

"I want to be part of his life."

This time, her agreement took a little longer in coming. She looked startled, as though she hadn't thought quite so far ahead.

"Well," she began.

"That's not up for debate." Later, when his thoughts weren't buzzing like wasps in a jar, he'd have to give some thought to how he could go from not knowing he had a son to insisting on a place in his son's life—all within the space of ten minutes. For now, all he knew was that boys needed fathers, and he planned to be a great one. Just because he'd missed the first several years of Jalen's life didn't mean he'd willingly miss any more. "Understand?"

A curt nod was his only answer.

Those details thus concluded, they stared at each other in shell-shocked silence.

Then some of his anger at being blindsided like this began to surface. It wasn't about the child or the money. It was about this woman he'd never seen before having the power to walk into his life and rearrange it, as though she'd swiped her hand across the chessboard, ruining a game well in progress.

"You'll want child support, I suppose."

Much to his surprise, she looked shocked. *"Child support?"*

Wow. She was good with the innocence and outrage. He'd have to remember that. "That's what this is about, isn't it? Money?"

"My God," she cried, "weren't you listening? I don't want your stupid money! I need your kidney!"

For the second time that day, the world dropped out from under him.

Healthy kids didn't need kidneys. Neither did mildly sick kids.

When he finally got his voice to work, it was an embarrassing croak. "What's wrong with him?"

"Jalen's in kidney failure."

The color bled out of Thomas's face, leaving it a sickly gray in jarring contrast to the brown of his throat.

After a second or two of indecision, he slipped into that medical zone and tried to take charge, the way that doctors do. That air of confidence used to reassure her back in the early days, but that was before she realized that, more often than not, doctors didn't know a damn thing about getting Jalen better.

"Polycystic kidney disease?" he demanded.

Like it mattered at this point. "No. He had a terrible case of E. Coli about two years ago, and that ruined his kidneys. Put him into kidney failure."

Undaunted, he plowed ahead. "Who's your doc? We've got a great specialist on staff—"

Was he for real? Or was it just that he couldn't comprehend a world where his larger-than-life medical connections and abilities didn't win the day? Whatever his issue was, Jalen was running out of time and she was way out of patience.

"We don't need a specialist. We have a specialist. Lots of them. And Jalen has been on dialysis for almost two years, and he's not doing well. Do you get that, Dr. Bradshaw? If I want my son to live—and I do—then I need to find him a compatible kidney quick, fast, and in a hurry, because my kidneys aren't a match, and neither are anyone's in my family. All of whom, by the way, live on the West Coast and have already been tested. And you'll have to forgive me if I don't want my son to sit on the transplant list for another two years, waiting for a match to materialize out of nowhere."

"But—"

Something inside her head snapped. Jalen was knocking pretty hard on death's door, and this fool wasn't coming up to speed fast enough. Hell, if she gave him another minute, maybe he'd start yammering about going back to square one and getting another opinion about whether Jalen had renal failure at all. Maybe he'd suggest a dose of amoxicillin to see if that got Jalen back on his feet.

Didn't he understand how hard she'd fought to get this far? Didn't he know that she was desperate and overwrought and had nowhere else to turn? What more did she have to do?

Losing it completely, she smacked her palms on top his desk and leaned down to get in his face. "Don't *but* me! My son is sick! He's going to die! Do you want me to beg? Is that it? Well, here it is. Help me. You're my only hope. You're my only hope! You're my only—"

"Okay." There was a flash of movement, and then, suddenly, he was on his feet, turning her to face him and grabbing her biceps to keep her from crumpling to the floor. The next thing she knew, he was in her face, instead of the other way around, soothing and reassuring. "Shhh, Lia," he murmured. "It's okay. You don't have to do this by yourself anymore. It's okay. I'll help you. It's okay."

Hysteria had her around the throat, ready to suck her under, but she gasped in a shaky breath and tried to hold it off. Just for a little while longer, until she was certain she'd heard right and wasn't getting her hopes up only so they could be smashed on the rocks.

"Y-you believe me?"

He stared at her and then, slowly, nodded.

"You'll be tested to see if you're a match?"

"If the DNA test first confirms that he's my son, then yes."

Could it be this easy? After all her struggles to get to this point?

She stared into his eyes, determined to root out any trickery.

There was none. Only his unwavering gaze, absolute and determined. And she knew, suddenly, that they had real hope now, she and Jalen. Better than that, they had a powerful ally. Thomas Bradshaw would help them in their fight against this terrible enemy, who had so many more resources than they did.

The relief was so sharp and overwhelming that her knees went squishy. A sob filled up her throat but not before she managed to whisper two words:

"Thank you."

Gratitude made her lose her head. Before she knew what she was doing, she was wrapping him in her arms, hugging him hard and trying to show how thankful she was, even if she couldn't say it. Naturally, he stiffened with shock, probably wondering if he should have his receptionist get security in there to kick Lia out after all.

Her cheeks burned hot with embarrassment as she got a grip. "Sorry," she muttered, easing up and ready to back away and let the poor man go. But then a strange thing happened.

Thomas hugged her back, gathering her in arms that were hard and strong and bringing her up against a broad chest, which was a lovely resting spot for her weary head. A croon rumbled in his throat, reassuring her without words, and the delicious warm scent of his skin, fresh from a recent shower, she thought, fogged her brain.

That was when reality intruded.

It had been years since she'd been pressed close to any man like this, and she wasn't immune to this particular man's appeal, even in her frazzled state. They fit together too well, and it shouldn't feel this good or this right to be chest to chest and thigh to thigh with someone she'd just met. Now was not the time for her dormant hormones to wake up and demand attention.

Coming to her senses, she pulled free and stepped back, catching a flash of turbulence, quickly managed and hidden, in his expression. They shifted awkwardly, fumbling with their limbs as though they'd each grown a new pair and didn't know quite how to work them, and then stared in opposite directions.

Finally, Thomas cleared his throat.

"So," he said, "there's a lab about a mile from here."

Her lungs loosened up, allowing her to breathe again. Medical tests and procedures were second nature to her, unlike dizzying hugs from sexy men. "Right. Should I take Jalen there for the paternity test?"

"Yeah. I'll arrange it."

"Great." Now that they were back in familiar territory, she risked a glance at his eyes, which was as jarring as a ten-foot drop in an elevator. Those brown eyes were way too intense and, for all she knew, saw too much.

And yet, she couldn't look away.

"Knock-knock, dearie." The receptionist tapped on the door and, without waiting for an answer, opened it and poked her head inside, providing just the snap back to reality that Lia needed. "Don't forget your staff meeting. We don't want this young lady with no manners to make you late, now, do we?"

Much to Lia's surprise, Thomas demonstrated the beginnings of a sense of humor and quirked a brow. "This young lady does need work with her manners, but she has a name, and we should probably use it. Lia Taylor, meet my receptionist, Mrs. Brennan."

The women exchanged reserved smiles and a grudging handshake, during which Mrs. Brennan's keen gaze skimmed over Lia from head to foot, probably noting everything from her choice in eye shadow to her suspected weight and shoe size. This examination culminated in Mrs. Brennan shooting a wry glance at Thomas.

"Well, she's a pretty little thing, isn't she, Doctor? And don't pretend you haven't noticed." A scowl crept across his face, flattening his brows and thinning his lips, but Mrs. Brennan seemed oblivious to this nonverbal warning and kept right on chirping. "I think I'll just have to keep my eye on this one, won't I?"

"Ah, Mrs. Brennan." Thomas's voice now had a steely edge. "You remember that discussion we had earlier, don't you?"

Mrs. Brennan waved a hand. "Oh, I'm not digging into your personal life. I'm simply noting, in passing, mind you, that there's something striking about wee Lia. You agree, don't you?" And without waiting for any answer, she waggled those fingers again and swept back up the hall.

Lia gaped after her. What the hell was the poor man supposed to say to *that?*

Thomas cleared his throat and quickly busied himself by straightening some files on his desk. "Sorry about that," he muttered. "Mrs. Brennan takes some, ah, getting used to, and I'm not sure—"

"It's okay." Lia shrugged and ducked her head as she started to leave, determined to get out of there before she either burst into tears again, or worse, her burning cheeks ignited. "I need to get back to work, anyway. I'll get out of your hair. Bye."

"Lia," he said sharply.

"Yes?"

"You didn't tell me…"

He hesitated, looking grim. He was allowed, she supposed; she'd dumped five tons of bricks on him in the last several minutes. Another of those endless beats passed between them, and she almost thought she saw color creep up his jaw from his neck. Was the arrogant surgeon feeling as flustered as she was right now? And why did it matter to her one way or the other?

"How can I stay in touch with you?" he asked.

Chapter 4

Thomas watched Lia go, straining his ears for any sound of her heels, long after she disappeared from view. There was some event he needed to go to pretty soon, he thought, but since his brain no longer seemed to be functional, he couldn't remember what it was. Rounds, right? Wait—no. Patients. He had appointments with patients, and then he— No. That wasn't it, either. He had a…meeting. A staff meeting. That was it. He should get going.

Except that stunned paralysis kept his ass stuck to his chair.

For the first time in living memory, possibly the first time ever, he didn't know what to do. Which was funny because he was a textbook type-A control freak who could handle whatever emergencies life threw his way. Need someone to head up the surgery department? He was your man. Need a surgeon to keep someone from bleeding out on the table? Look no further. Need a physician to teach, publish and cook a mean three-course dinner in his spare time? Right here, pal.

A crisis in someone else's life was a piece of cake.

A crisis in his own life was a whole 'nother kettle of stinking fish.

Jesus.

What on earth was he supposed to do now?

Why couldn't he get his thoughts to coalesce into something coherent? Something other than:

I have a son. I have a son with Lia. Our son could die.

There was no room for *might, possibly* or *could.*

I might *have a son.* Uh-uh. That didn't work for him at all.

He had a son. Period. End of story.

And that was another thing. He hadn't signed up for this. He'd been minding his own business, doing his own thing, not looking to be a daddy, so why did he now feel excitement at the idea of meeting the boy and terror at the idea of him being so sick?

Was he insane? Had all his marbles suddenly been lost?

He'd had a fatherhood scare once, about three years ago. A condom had ripped. While he'd tried not to hyperventilate with panic at the idea of being saddled with a kid at that point in his life, not to mention that particular girlfriend as a baby mama, she'd chattered happily about their future together if she was pregnant. He'd sweated bullets until she got her period, and then he'd answered the wake-up call and said his goodbyes, because she wasn't the one and never would have been the one. That wasn't the time. He hadn't been ready.

Not that he was ready now. Of course he wasn't ready.

No way.

Even if there was that unaccountable excitement surging inside him.

But he couldn't go off all half-cocked. He probably should see about getting a lawyer and—

That was it! Max. He needed Max.

Snatching up his cell phone, he dialed the number, wishing for the billionth time, that Max Wade, his roommate from Dartmouth undergrad lived closer to Alexandria than NYC. It'd be nice to have this discussion over a Scotch and a steak after work, rather than in a hurried phone call.

Anyway, Max would help him out. He had the cold-blooded shrewdness of a great white shark and the sentimentality that polar bears feel for sea lions. Max would talk some sense into him or die trying.

"Maxwell Wade, attorney-at-law," said Max in his ear after the third ring. "Speak to me. My time is money and you're already up to eighty-five dollars for this phone call."

Typical. "You're full of shit, Wade, you know that? I'm wondering, does it squish in your shoes when you walk?"

Max laughed. "The answer to that question will cost you another eighty-five. It's up to you."

Emotion tightened down Thomas's throat, making it hard for him to get the words out. Plus, saying it would make it real, and God knew, he wasn't ready for that.

On the other hand, if he was a father, he'd need to step up to the plate.

"I've got a situation," he said.

The smile left Max's voice. "Sounds serious."

"I…think I have an eight-year-old son."

"Oh, shit, man."

"That about sums it up, yeah."

Max whooshed out a breath. "How do you know?"

"The boy's mother told me—"

"Hold up. You can't take somebody's word for that, Tommy. You know that."

"I know."

"Have you had a DNA test yet?"

"Not yet. But I'm going to."

"Yeah, well, in the meantime, you keep your mouth shut, you hear? You don't sign anything, you don't admit to anything and you don't—"

For reasons that eluded him at the moment, Thomas found himself getting irritated. "Look, man, I'm not trying to weasel out of my responsibilities here."

"Your *alleged* responsibilities. Got it? *Alleged.* And until that test comes back saying you're the one, all you have is some woman's word for it. And you better believe she knows how much money you have, and she wants to get paid. So, you just cool it for now."

"I've seen the boy, man. He looks just like me."

It sounded like Max was choking with outrage. "I didn't raise you to be that stupid, man. Please tell me you didn't meet the kid, and now you think he's all cute, like a puppy and shit—"

"Of course not. But his picture looks just like me at that age."

"One word, man. Photoshop."

These were all good points, and this was exactly the kind of advice he'd hoped to hear when he dialed Max's number. So why did the brother's doubts about Lia and her motives make him want to reach through the phone and jam his fist down Max's throat?

"She's not a gold digger," he said flatly. "I know."

"Oh, you know." Max snorted with derisive laughter. "How do you know?"

"Because I can feel it." The words came out strong and sure, even though Thomas knew how crazy all this was. *He could feel it.* Oh, really? Please. But he *could* feel it, even if he couldn't explain it. If there was one thing he knew about Lia Taylor with utter certainty, it was that. "And the boy's in renal failure."

"Oh, no." Max gasped with shock, and Thomas could see him shaking his head and then resting his forehead on his hands. He appreciated the sympathy. "God help you."

"Yeah," Thomas agreed grimly. "God help all three of us."

"Ready for bed?" Lia asked.

She hovered in Jalen's doorway, trying to get a bead on his mood at the moment. He was generally resigned to going to bed at nine o'clock, but every now and then he pitched a fit and wanted extra time for whatever computerizing he was doing on her MacBook. The kid had inherited a double dose of her technology skills and loved anything with a memory card in it, which had its ups and downs. His grades were great, and she was always safe in getting him the latest gadget for

Christmas, but the downside was she lived in fear of an irate call from the CIA claiming that he'd hacked into their spy satellite system or some such.

Tonight, though, the computer was open but untouched, and that worried her.

Bustling inside, she worked on keeping her voice upbeat. "Jammies? Check. Showered?" She sniffed under his arm for deodorant. "Check. You just need to brush your teeth, and you'll be good to go."

Jalen was a devoted Trekkie. Today's pajama selection was a black knit set with white writing that proclaimed him a Future Starship Captain, and he was collapsed against his USS Enterprise pillows. Unfortunately, he looked worse than he had a mere hour ago at dinner, and seemed drawn and exhausted, barely able to keep his lids from drooping.

Lia's heart sank because they'd lost ground again today, and Jalen's weakening body was that much closer to killing him.

They were always losing ground, never gaining it, which was why she'd been driven to desperate acts, like hacking into sperm-donor databases. There were times, like now, when she wondered if he'd fade or wither away right before her eyes. In the old days, before he got sick, he'd relished this computer time. His fingers would fly over the keyboard, tapping out God knew what at a rate of about ninety words per minute. Not lately, though. Not for a while. She'd started dreading tomorrows, because each one took a little bit more out of her boy, and she didn't know how many he'd have left if he didn't get a new kidney soon.

Still, his personality was alive and well inside that

failing body. His brows scrunched so low over his fore-head that it was a wonder she could see his scowling eyes.

Eyes that were, she now knew, exactly like his father's.

"It's pajamas, Mom," he informed her. "Not jam-mies."

"Pardon me." She nudged aside a couple of LEGO spaceships that he'd assembled, disassembled and reas-sembled approximately 1.5 million times and sat on the edge of his bed. "Why have you not engaged in your nightly computer gaming, young sir?"

He grunted. "Like it matters."

She rolled her eyes and bit back a sharp reply, hanging on to her crucial serenity by a slender thread. Whoever said that eight-year-olds were too young for hormone surges was a damn liar. On the other hand, if ever a kid had a reason to be occasionally sullen, this one did. Renal failure and dialysis did that to a person.

She gave him a critical once-over. He was thinner. Always thinner. When he wasn't retaining water, that was. He hadn't eaten much of the homemade chicken nuggets she'd served him at dinner. But his blood pres-sure had been fine earlier, so that was one good thing.

Which left only ninety-nine thousand, nine hundred and ninety-nine other items to keep her from getting any sleep.

"Were you editing today's video?" Under the guise of snuggling, she wrapped an arm around his shoul-der and leaned in close to press a lingering kiss to his temple. Oh, thank goodness. He didn't feel warm at all. She was always worried about an infection developing around his access.

"Mom!" Squirming away, Jalen nailed her with a weak glower. "I don't have a fever, okay? Jeez."

"Oops," she said, stung that the little stinker could read her so easily. "Well, sorrr-yyy. I need to check. It's my job."

Apparently exhausted by the effort it took to wage a protest, he slumped back against the pillows. "And I don't have any swelling or redness around my access, either. Okay? So I don't need an inspection. Thank you!"

He huffed, exchanging a can-you-believe-that look of deepest disgust with Bones, his ten-pound floppy-eared bunny, who occupied his usual place of honor in the basket on the nightstand. Bones twitched his nose in seeming sympathy with Jalen's plight, scratched at his black collar with a powerful hind leg and then went back to systematically shredding his fleece blanket with his massive front teeth.

Okay, Lia, she told herself. *Try not to be such a helicopter parent. Don't let your rotors show.*

Letting Jalen go, she stretched out beside him and focused on the video he hadn't had the energy to edit. In today's episode of *The Bunny Chronicles*, downloaded fresh from the pet-cam Bones habitually wore around his neck, the rabbit hopped around the house and explored the space behind the living-room sofa, nibbled the fringe on the Navajo rug in Lia's bedroom and shredded and ate a small piece of paper that had fallen to the side of Lia's desk.

"Is that the Walmart receipt for the sheets I bought last week?" she wondered, squinting at the screen for a closer look. "I've been looking for that."

"Bones strikes again," Jalen murmured.

"How come he never eats any of your stuff?"

"Training, Mom." His voice was growing fainter; she'd lose him to sleep soon. "It's all about the training."

Laughing, Lia got to her feet and stretched. "I'm going to throw another load in the washing machine, okay? You need to brush your teeth."

Weary eye roll. "Okay."

"Which episode of *Star Trek* are we watching tonight? Original or *The Next Generation*?"

What he said next really scared her.

"I'm too tired. I'm going to go to sleep."

She cleared her throat, struggling against the rising fear. "Okay," she said, but it wasn't okay, because Jalen was slipping away from life.

No. She wouldn't go there. Never allowed herself to go there.

The phone rang from somewhere in his room, jarring her away from the absolute blackness of her thoughts, thank God. She turned to look for it on the nightstand, but he was already fishing it out from under one of his pillows.

"What's the phone doing there?"

Jalen, who'd recently discovered the delights of both making and answering phone calls and had a real fondness for calling her cell phone four or five times per day just to see what she was doing, dimpled drowsily and then answered.

"Taylor residence." His voice had gone deep and impressive, as though he had been appointed receptionist for the president. "State your business."

"Jalen!" Lia cried.

He ignored this interruption. "Who's calling, please?" He listened, frowning thoughtfully. Then he lowered the phone and spoke to her in a stage whisper, which could probably be heard for miles around. "Do we know a Thomas Bradshaw?"

Stifling a gasp at the realization that Jalen was talking to his real father for the first time and didn't know it, she held her hand out. "I'll take it. You brush your teeth."

"Fine." Grumbling, Jalen slowly got up and headed for the bathroom.

Lia, meanwhile, hurried down the hall and into the kitchen, terrified that Jalen would experience one of his eerie bursts of near omniscience and figure out what was going on way before she was ready to tell him. Along the way, she passed umpteen framed pictures of Alan on the wall, each one lovingly placed years ago so that Alan would never be forgotten and Jalen would feel like he knew his "father."

How was that for irony?

Why did sudden guilt threaten to swallow her whole? Because Alan was dead and she was about to displace his memory from Jalen's life? Or was it because she was still young and alive and had felt a powerful sexual attraction to Jalen's real father?

The pictures seemed to accuse her, so she did her best to avoid looking directly at any of them. She knew them by heart, anyway: Alan laughing and holding the massive fish he'd caught during their honeymoon in St. John's, Alan playing catcher during a softball game with some of his buddies, Alan grinning over her swollen belly during her ultrasound the day they'd found out they were expecting a son.

Good thing they hadn't had a crystal ball on that joyous day.

What would they have done if they'd known that Alan would die before he ever saw Jalen's face? Or that Jalen could well die before his ninth birthday?

Jalen.

How the hell was she supposed to tell him the truth about his biological father?

"Yes," she said into the phone. Jittery with nerves, she cleared her throat and tried again. "I mean hello. It's Lia."

"Am I catching you at a bad time?"

Oh, man. There was something deliciously intimate about Thomas's low voice in her ear, something illicit, and she had no business wondering where he was at this hour or who he might be with.

Stick to business, Lia.

"No. I'm just putting Jalen in bed. What's up?"

"I, ah, just wanted to check in. So that was him answering the phone, huh?"

So that quick but momentous exchange hadn't been lost on Thomas, either, had it? The thought unsettled her. Thrilled her. Funny how she'd spent all this time and effort finding Jalen's father in the hopes that he could be a kidney donor and save the boy's life, and yet had given little, if any, thought to the effect this revelation would have on both males.

Well. She was thinking about it now, that was for sure.

"That was him."

"He, ah…" Thomas trailed off, clearly in a struggle

with his thoughts, words or emotions or possibly all three. After a long pause, he tried again. "He's got a sense of humor on him, doesn't he?"

That made her smile. "You have no idea."

Another silence. She waited, wondering where this conversation was going and when, if ever, the great Dr. Bradshaw had been this uncertain about anything in his life.

"So... His blood pressure's okay?"

"I'll check it again, before he goes to bed. He's getting pretty sick of me hovering, though."

"He's a kid. You can't blame him for that."

"I know."

"I stopped by the lab on the way home and gave a tissue sample. We should hear in a day or two."

"Wow." This time tomorrow, then, Jalen would have an official father and she would no longer be his only parent. Astonishing. Terrifying. Lia leaned against the counter, fighting against the sudden knot of anxiety in her belly. "That's pretty fast."

"Yeah," he agreed on a long, shaky breath. "Pretty fast."

More silence. Lia shifted back and forth on her feet, waiting for him to say whatever seemed to be on the tip of his tongue, needing something that she couldn't quite identify—something from him.

What was it? Absolution? Understanding? Or worse, something that had nothing to do with Jalen at all and everything to do with the humming electricity she felt when she interacted with Thomas?

"Well," he said finally, "I'll let you go."

Good. Great. Ending this disturbing conversation

was the best thing to do. Yes. And while she was at it, she should work on remembering that she and Thomas would soon be something like business partners, nothing more. Two strangers united in the business of saving and raising the world's greatest boy. End of story.

Which meant that the niggling disappointment she felt was ridiculous. The man had already gone above and beyond the call of duty by taking time out of his busy day to check on a kid who was, as yet, no official relation to him.

What more did she expect?

"Right. Well… Have a good night, then."

"Lia."

The new urgency in his voice took her aback. "Yes?"

"How are you doing?"

Huh? What kind of random question was that? Automatically, all her defenses went up. "I'm fine. I'm not the one who's sick," she reminded him, bristling at even the suggestion of weakness. Hadn't she raised Jalen all by herself while working full time lo these many years? Did he think she was incapable? Was that it? "Why would you ask about me?"

"Because, Superwoman," he said softly, and there was something surprising in his tone now, something almost like tenderness, "someone needs to look out for you while you're looking out for Jalen."

"In here, Jay," Lia said two days later, steering Jalen through the outer door and into the reception area of Thomas's deserted office suite. "We'll have a seat right here."

Jalen, whose thin shoulders were tight as harp strings, surveyed the room—the sleek glass tables, gray chairs and oversize and moody black-and-white landscape photos. She couldn't blame him for being tense. Having spent way too much of his short life in medical settings, she didn't expect him to be bouncing with joy over the thrill of visiting yet another doctor's office, even if he wasn't there as a patient.

She, on the other hand, was tense for altogether different reasons, and had been since she'd received Thomas's terse phone call a little while ago.

"Come to my office," he'd said. "I've got the paternity-test results."

Though she knew they were coming and had, in fact, been waiting breathlessly for this very call, it suddenly seemed way too soon. "But—" she spluttered.

"Bring the boy," Thomas said, and hung up.

Arrogant SOB, she thought now, settling onto one of the chairs and crossing her legs. Snapping his fingers. Expecting her to jump. Calling Jalen "the boy." Who the hell did he think he was?

The answer came immediately:

Jalen's only hope, that's who.

"I still don't get why we're here." Jalen, no doubt tired by the long walk from the parking garage, slumped into a chair and rifled through a stack of magazines, scrunching his nose at *Newsweek, Essence,* and *Vanity Fair.* "Why do I have to come if this isn't my doctor— Ooh, *Spider-Man.* Cool. How long is this going to take?"

What could she say? *Well, Jalen, we'll be here long*

enough for me to explain that everything I've told you about your father up until now is a lie.

Luckily she was saved by Mrs. Brennan, who emerged from the inner depths of the suite, appeared on the other side of the glass window and slid it open.

"Well, well, well," she said, placing a stack of files on her desk and thereby freeing up her hands so she could place them on her broad hips and hit Lia with a wry smile. "If it isn't Miss Lia of the No Manners, come to visit us again. And who might this fine young man be? Oh." The smile dimmed, leaving open astonishment as she studied Jalen with those keen blue eyes, which, as Lia had feared, saw everything around her with high-def clarity. *"Oh."*

Jalen looked up from his comic book and waved. "Hey."

"Hey," Mrs. Brennan said faintly.

"Mrs. Brennan," Lia said loudly, giving the woman a significant look over Jalen's head and praying she wouldn't prematurely let any cats out of their bags. "This is Jalen, my son."

With difficulty, Mrs. Brennan peeled her slack-jawed gaze away from Jalen and turned her attention back to Lia, much to Lia's consternation. There was way too much kindness in the woman's smile now, too much understanding. It made Lia's throat tighten and her heart contract, and the emotion was only intensified when Mrs. Brennan spoke again.

"Yes, lass." Those bright eyes sparkled with tears now, which Mrs. Brennan briskly swiped away. "I see exactly whose son this is."

Oh, God.

Lia blinked furiously, determined not to lose it any sooner than she needed to.

Jalen cocked his head, his bemused gaze flickering between the women.

Mrs. Brennan reached for a massive candy jar off to the side of her desk and lifted the lid with a flourish. "Tell me, young Mr. Jalen, can you help me put a dent in these chocolates here? I've got way too many of the peanut butter ones left. We'd better do something about that."

Jalen was already on the move. "I try to help when I can."

The two bent their heads low and murmured over the selection while Lia dabbled at her eyes with a tissue fished out of the pocket of her skirt. She was beginning to feel marginally better—more in control, at least—when Mrs. Brennan's desk phone beeped and she leaned around Jalen to look at Lia with the same empathy that had just unraveled her.

"Dr. Bradshaw will see you now."

"Great," Lia said, even though the words made her heart stutter and stop dead. Thomas would see her now. And then what? What if he wasn't Jalen's father after all? What if he was? What would she do either way?

And then, somehow, she was on her feet, and her feet were moving, and she was passing first through the door next to the receptionist's window and then through the inner door to Thomas's office, which he held open for her.

He stared at her with the hard-jawed, icy-eyed gaze he'd used on poor Dr. Brown the other day, and it was all she could do to stand straight and proud and wait for him to utter the words that would change her life, one way or the other.

"Jalen's my son." Hesitating, he struggled with the words. "He's…*our* son."

"Okay." Lia tried to say something else, floundered and lapsed into silence as she sank into a chair. She looked a little green around the gills, which was exactly how Thomas felt. "So that's that, then. Wow."

Wow. Yeah, that about summed it up.

Because he didn't know what else to do, he walked back around his desk and resumed his spot in his leather chair, hoping the seat would provide him with a little clarity and help him think. It didn't. All he knew was that, on the other side of that wall right there, was an eight-year-old boy who was his flesh and blood, and Thomas now needed to step up to the plate and become a father, armed only with the pathetic skills he'd learned from his own less-than-stellar daddy dearest, the Admiral.

Poor Jalen. The kid probably thought that renal failure was the scariest issue facing him right now. If he only knew.

Lia sat there, staring off in the distance, her eyes unfocused. Her sudden silence really ticked him off. She had set this snowball rolling down the mountain in the first place, culminating in an avalanche that obliterated the carefully structured life he'd worked for and earned up until now. His anger was irrational, he knew, but he couldn't help it.

"Why so quiet, Lia? Or should I call you Baby Mama? Cat got your tongue?"

She leveled a glare on him that announced she was gunning for a fight, just like he was. Which suited him fine.

"I need a minute," she told him. "We need to think this through."

Oh, she was funny.

"Think this through? I thought you had all the answers already, Lia. Or did I miss something?" He paused, drawing it out just to be as obnoxious as possible. "Let's recap, just to be sure. You illegally hacked into private sperm-donor records without being prosecuted, tracked me down and now have DNA proof that I'm the father of your son. So now I'm going to be screened for donor compatibility this afternoon. You didn't think I was a big enough bastard to refuse to be tested, did you? And hopefully soon you'll have a kidney for your son, which is everything you wanted and schemed for. Doesn't that about cover it? So what's the big deal? What's to think through?"

Her cheeks were a bright and angry red, telling him she didn't care for this version of the facts. "Well, for one thing, what I did wasn't as Machiavellian as that—"

"Wasn't it?"

"—and for another thing, I don't know how to tell Jalen who you are. I was so worried about finding you that I didn't think too much about what would happen when I did."

"Shocking. Do you mean to tell me this brilliant plan of yours has a flaw?"

"Can we do this without the sarcasm?" she asked quietly.

"Probably not."

Scooting to the edge of her chair, she rested her palms down on his desk, beseeching him. "You may not believe this, but I'm trying my hardest for my son."

"*Our* son."

"I don't have all the answers. Half the time, I don't think I have any of the answers. All I know is that I have to fight for him, because if I don't, who will?"

I will, he started to say, but he wasn't ready for that. Not yet.

Nor was he ready to acknowledge that this crusading warrior was exactly the kind of mother he'd've chosen for his kid. If he'd ever been given the chance to decide for himself. But he hadn't because she'd ripped that opportunity away from him, hadn't she?

"What do you want me to say?" He wondered. "That what you did is all right?"

"No." She hesitated. "Yes. I want you to understand. I want you to forgive me."

"Oh. Is that all?"

"Do you want me to apologize? Is that it?"

He couldn't say *yes*, but he couldn't say *no*, either.

His ambivalence seemed to unhinge her a little. "Well, I'm sorry, O Great Surgeon," she cried. "I'm sorry I've upset your thrilling career and your perfect carefree life with my sick son. But this was about saving Jalen! It wasn't about you!"

"Well, it's about me now."

The deathly calm in his voice made her flinch. The blood leached out of her cheeks, leaving her pale and scared. "What does that mean?"

"It means that I'm going to be involved in my boy's life."

"You don't have to. No one expects it."

"I do have to, because I expect it."

That stumped her for a minute, and then she treated him to the ghost of a dimpled smile, which was like the hint of a rainbow hiding behind a cloud. "So you have honor, then, Thomas?"

"Yes," he admitted. "Much to my surprise."

They stared at each other, the desk serving as a no-man's-land between them.

Lia spoke first, her voice shaky with nerves. "What does that mean, that you want to be involved in his life? Explain that to me."

As if he knew. Still, he gave it a stab, listing some of the things his father had never done with him. "I want to tuck him in at night. I want to read him stories and play Monopoly with him. We need to go fishing and play hoops. I want to pay for his food and his clothes and his toys. I'll be in on the decisions about his medical care." Sudden emotion tightened his throat, choking off the words. "And if God gives me the chance, I want to teach him to shave and to drive and pay for his college." He blinked, trying to hold back the hot tears that wanted to fall and unman him. The image of the Admiral's disapproval over such a display of emotion helped him suck it up and hold it together. "That about sums it up. For now."

Lia shook her head with visible alarm. "Are you trying to take my place? Is that it?"

"Of course not," he said, but the reassuring words didn't quite match the simmering anger inside him. It wasn't Lia's fault—he kept reminding himself of that— but she'd been there from the beginning, and Thomas hadn't. She'd seen their son's first smile, step and every other first in the boy's life, and what had Thomas seen? What had he had? Nothing. And if he wasn't a kidney match and they couldn't find a kidney match, he might never have anything of Jalen except for bitter regret over what might have been. "But I do want a place in his life. A big place."

"I see." The desk might have been a battlefield between them, and their gazes met, his furious, hers sad but resolute. "So the bottom line is, you hate me for bringing Jalen into your life and also hate me for having eight years with him when you've had none."

Wonderful. She was beautiful, brilliant, tough and intuitive. Was there a more lethal combination? Maybe he should just surrender right now. Clearly, he didn't have a snowball's chance of holding his own against this woman or her son.

Did he hate her?

He thought about trying to sugarcoat his response, but what was the point?

"At this moment?" he said. "Yeah. I hate you."

She took it like a woman, her lips twisting into a wry smile. "You do realize how illogical that is, don't you?"

"Absolutely."

"Any other hard feelings I should know about? Before we get this thing started?"

He hesitated, but, hey, they were being honest, right? Wasn't honesty the best policy? "Yeah." He held her gaze, letting her see more of him than he showed anyone else, which was terrifying and exhilarating. Funny, wasn't it? Since he'd laid eyes on Lia two days ago, he'd felt more supercharged than he ever had in his life.

"I'm not wild about the way you've wormed your way into my head."

She stilled, her breath catching with a little hitch. "Me and Jalen, you mean."

"No," he said softly. "I mean you."

She flushed prettily. He watched her, thinking that if they weren't in the middle of a crisis here, he could spend a lot more time studying the reactions of that face, the sparkle of those brown eyes and the things that made her laugh, so he could do them and see those dimples and that smile much more often.

To his astonishment, she got up, smoothed her skirt and came around the desk toward him.

Frozen with anticipation, he had a tough time getting his voice to work. "What're you doing?"

She stopped right there, right in front of him, ignoring all social etiquette and perching on the edge of his desk, close enough for him to smell the spicy warmth of her skin. He stared up at her, mesmerized and keeping his twitchy hands to himself only with supreme difficulty.

"I'm tired of being intimidated by you sitting behind this big desk and scared of your reactions and worried about what you might or might not agree to do and how you feel about me. We're equals as far as I'm concerned. Just two scared parents trying to do the right thing for their son. And since we're both mature adults— You are a mature adult, aren't you, Doctor?"

That made him smile. "Most days, yeah."

"Oh, good. Since we're both mature adults, I think we can find a way to work together, don't you?"

With Lia looking at him, her brown eyes bright with

earnest hope and a tiny bit of trust and faith, there was no way he could tell her anything other than, "Yes. We can work together."

Wordlessly, she held out her hand.

They shook, her soft, warm palm sliding against his and squeezing with surprising strength, and there was that supercharged thrill again. He felt the unaccountable certainty that, with Lia nearby, the world was opening up to him in a way it never had before. And then, too soon, she was pulling free and cold reality was back again, smacking them in the face.

"Are you as scared as I am, Thomas?" she wondered aloud.

"Hell, yeah."

She nodded, looking reassured for some reason. "Ready to meet your son now?"

Finally, an easy question.

"Hell, yeah."

Oh, man.

Thomas looked down at his long-fingered hands, the ones that could move quickly and deftly with a scalpel, performing bypasses, repairing aneurisms, excising cancers and generally saving lives under the direst possible conditions.

They were shaking.

That's right, sports fans. He, Thomas Bradshaw, IV, M.D., son of a decorated naval admiral, head of surgery at a major hospital and fearless cardiothoracic surgeon, was scared shitless at the prospect of meeting an eight-year-old boy.

His eight-year-old boy.

He paced the office, waiting while Lia brought Jalen in and giving himself pointers on how to play it cool and not freak the kid out any more than necessary. First off, Lia had said that the whole desk thing was intimidating, so he wouldn't sit there.

Second, to hug or not to hug? Did kids that age want hugs? What were the father-son rules regarding affection? Well, he knew what the Admiral's single rule was: no displays of affection under any circumstances. But that wasn't a model he wanted to use for his own father-son relationship. So, he'd be flexible on the whole hug thing. Read Jalen's cues.

And what about spending time with the kid? What did he like to do? Did he have hobbies? Why the hell hadn't he asked Lia about that when he'd had the chance a minute ago? How soon should they start hanging out togeth—

There was a light tap, and then the door swung open and a smiling Lia walked in, tugging Jalen by the hand behind her. The second he saw him, all Thomas's best intentions did a suicide jump right out the window, leaving him slack jawed and staring.

Jalen.

His son.

He was thin but tall for his age, all dangling arms and long legs. He wore jeans, gym shoes and a white T-shirt with black lettering: *Beam Me Up, Mr. Sulu.* Cool. The kid was a Trekkie; Thomas could respect that. His brown skin was fairer than Thomas's, more like Lia's, and his expression was wary. The hair rose all up and down Thomas's arms because he might have been meeting a ghost—the ghost of his eight-year-old self.

Eerie didn't even begin to describe the sensation.

Lia and Jalen came closer, and that was when Thomas's medical training took over. This was the same kid from the picture he'd seen the other day, with the same big brown eyes, plump lips and straight nose, but this was no picture of health standing in front of him.

Not even close.

Jalen's head seemed way too big for those thin shoulders. His eyes, though bright, had that sunken and hollowed look Thomas remembered too well from his pediatric rotation during his residency. And his face was a little puffy, making him worry about fluid retention.

This kid was, in a word, sick.

Deathly sick.

Thomas studied his son and felt his heart swell and break a million times over.

"Dude," Jalen said after a few seconds. "You're staring at me."

Thomas choked off a surprised snort of laughter, but Lia rounded on the boy.

"Jalen! What have I told you about calling adults *dude?*"

Jalen huffed with irritation over this unfairness. "Well, he is staring at me!"

Lia rolled her eyes and shot Thomas a look of deepest exasperation. "Dr. Thomas Bradshaw, this is Jalen. Jalen, Dr. Bradshaw."

Thomas quickly held out his hand and they shook. The boy's grip was nice and strong and seemed cool enough for Thomas to rule out fever or infection. For now, anyway.

"Nice to—" Thomas's voice squeaked, so he had to stop, clear his throat and try again. "Nice to meet you, Jalen."

"You, too." Jalen cocked his head and locked Thomas in his sights, doing a little staring of his own. "You look familiar to me."

Jesus. This little guy didn't miss a trick, did he? The more he spoke, the more Thomas doubted whether he was up to the task of raising someone so precocious.

"Ah," he stammered. "Familiar? You think so?"

"Sorta." Jalen now regarded him with solemn eyes and, luckily, changed the subject. "I'm in trouble, right?"

"No," Thomas said, startled. "Of course not. What makes you think that?"

"Oh, great." Jalen folded his arms over his chest, glaring at them with open suspicion now. "So you're going to stick me with another needle, then, right? I knew it."

"No, Jalen," Thomas said. "We just want to talk to you."

Jalen looked to Lia for confirmation.

She nodded.

"Then why are you both acting funny and staring at me?" Jalen demanded.

"Well, this is important, honey." Lia steered them toward the sofa beneath the window, where they all sat with Jalen in the middle. "We want to make sure we do a good job explaining everything to you."

"I'm not dumb," Jalen told her.

"Duh," Lia said. "I think I know that by now."

Jalen swiveled to face Thomas. "Maybe he thinks I'm dumb."

Thomas swallowed his laughter, which was hard, and worked on maintaining the appropriate solemnity. "Listen, buddy. I can assure you that I don't think you're dumb. At all."

"I get all *A*s in school," Jalen informed him.

"That doesn't surprise me," Thomas said, keeping a tight grip on his smile.

Mollified that the adults were taking him seriously at last, Jalen settled back against the leather cushions and got comfortable. "Well, what is it, then? What's going on?"

Thomas looked to Lia.

Lia looked back, a distinct flare of panic in her eyes.

Not knowing what else to do, he gave her a tiny wink. Much to his surprise, it seemed to work, and her lips curved a little with something that might have been gratitude. Taking a deep breath, she turned to Jalen and put her arm around him.

"It's about your father," she said.

Jalen's mouth rounded open with surprise. "My father?"

"Yes." Lia hesitated, choosing her words carefully. "You know that your daddy and I were married, and we wanted a child very much, and we tried really hard to have you. And then I got pregnant, and we were so thrilled."

"And then Daddy died," Jalen said.

"Yes. And then he died. But the thing I never mentioned, because you probably weren't old enough to understand—"

Jalen frowned, apparently not liking where this was going. "I'm old enough now!"

"Yes." Lia rubbed his shoulders, never missing a beat. "You're old enough now to understand that your daddy had some health issues and he wasn't able to help me make a baby."

Jalen cringed. "This is about eggs and sperms and stuff, isn't it?"

"Well, yes," Lia admitted.

Jalen looked revolted. "Oh, God."

"Gosh," Lia corrected. "So...the thing is...Daddy's sperm didn't work the way it was supposed to, but we still wanted a baby, so we had to find someone to donate sperm for us so we could make a baby. Does that make sense?"

Jalen's eyes blinked, and then they slid out of focus, staring off at nothing.

They waited. Thomas didn't know how Lia was doing, but his thundering heart felt like it was seconds away from full cardiac arrest. Good thing they were in a hospital, he thought in a burst of wild hysteria.

Slowly, Jalen turned to Thomas, looking like a bewildered little kid now, somehow smaller and younger than he'd been mere seconds ago.

"Jalen?" Lia tried gently.

The males both ignored her. At this moment, they only had eyes for each other.

"Are you my daddy?" Jalen whispered.

The question was way above Thomas's pay grade. Not the mechanics of it. That was easy. *Yeah, sure, kid, I'm the guy who jacked off in a cup so your mother could use my sperm.* The issue was the word *daddy*.

Daddy meant something far beyond genetics, even if Jalen was too young to realize the distinction, and Thomas hadn't earned the right to use it.

Not yet, anyway. But he would. He wasn't about to stare into this little guy's earnest face and make promises he couldn't deliver. Nor would he run roughshod over Jalen's dreams or deny this precious soul the basic affection and emotional support he deserved, the way the Admiral had done to him.

No freaking way.

He may not know what it meant to be a daddy—a good daddy—but he was about to make it his business to find out.

So he took a deep breath and put a steady hand on Jalen's shoulder.

"Yeah," he said. "I'm your daddy, and I want to be part of your life. I hope that's okay with you."

Jalen stilled, emotions tracking across his face so quickly that Thomas couldn't keep up. Hope, maybe? Confusion? Excitement? Betrayal? There might have been a hint of pain there as well, and Thomas felt a parent's anguish, just that quick. From now on, it would be his life's mission to do right by this kid and never hurt him if he could help it. To be there when he said he would…to teach…to protect. Whatever this kid needed, Thomas would get for him.

Including—especially—his kidney.

Jalen's brow crinkled, and then he confronted Lia, demanding her input. "Is he my daddy, Mommy?"

Lia nodded. "Yes, baby."

Jalen stiffened, and when he turned back to Thomas this time, there was anger in those big eyes. Accusation.

"Where have you been?" he demanded. "Don't you know that little kids need fathers?"

Thomas's heart broke, spreading pain from his chest to the farthest corners of his soul. He knew that kids tended to do that to you, but he hadn't thought it would happen quite this soon or be this excruciating. His mouth opened, but there were no words anywhere to be found.

The impotent silence didn't help his case any. Jalen's face twisted with eight-year-old fury as he ran out of patience and began to yell.

"Where have you been? Where have you been?"

There'd be time enough for explanations later. For now, there was only one thing this kid needed to hear. "I'm sorry, Jalen—"

"Where have you been?"

"—but I'm here now. And I'm not going anywhere. I'm not—"

There was a flurry of arms and a sparkle of tears. The next thing Thomas knew, Jalen was throwing himself across the sofa, wrapping his skinny arms around Thomas's middle in a death grip and laying his head on his chest. For one second of breathless astonishment, he caught sight of Lia's smile and her emotion, which mirrored his own, and then it hit him:

Your son is hugging you. Hug him back, stupid.

With difficulty, he extracted his arms and wrapped them around Jalen, holding him as tight and pulling him as close as he could manage. There was strength in the boy's body, unexpected strength, and his skin was soft, his weight heavier than he'd thought.

Thomas kissed his forehead and then, when he didn't

protest or wipe it away, kissed him again. Across the top of the boy's head, he looked to Lia again, and they laughed because they were both crying and couldn't think of one thing that needed to be said right now.

As Lia reached out to squeeze Thomas's arm in a silent offer of support and approval, he thought he could stay right there, just like this, forever.

Chapter 5

It didn't take Jalen long to tire of the emotional display and launch into full, inquisitive kid mode. This, of course, left the adults scrambling to dab their wet eyes and switch gears to keep up with him.

Lia sat and watched the interchange between father and son, grateful that she was not, for once, the object of all that unbridled energy.

Jalen sat up straight and got right to business. "So are you going to live with us?"

"Ah, no." Thomas quickly scooted back, clearly anxious to follow Jalen's cues and give him space when he needed it. Lia awarded him a silent *A* for effort and attentiveness. "I have my own house. It's not far from here. Maybe you can come visit sometimes. When we get to know each other a little better."

"Do you have other kids?"

"No."

"A dog?"

"No."

"A wife or anything?"

Lia's ears perked up, waiting for the answer to that question.

"No," Thomas said. "Just me."

"Oh." Jalen frowned thoughtfully. "That's pretty lonely."

"Ah, well…" Thomas's cheeks colored as his self-conscious gaze flickered to Lia and back to Jalen again. "I spend a lot of time working, so I, you know, didn't want to have a pet at home waiting for me all the time."

"Yeah, but if you don't have a pet, then you don't have anyone waiting for you. That's sad."

Thomas blinked.

"So you're a doctor, right?" Jalen continued. "Do you take care of kids like me with bad kidneys?"

"No. I'm a surgeon, so I—"

"I know what surgeons do." Jalen flapped an impatient hand. "I told you I'm smart. Are you neuro-, cardio- or plastic?"

"Ah…" Thomas looked so flabbergasted and tongue-tied that Lia almost felt sorry for him at this point. Almost. "Cardiothoracic."

"Do you like *Star Trek?* Can you do this?" Jalen held up one palm and arranged his fingers into a *V* for the Vulcan salute. "Live Long and Prosper."

Thomas stared at him for three long beats, looking dazed. And then he raised his hand and repeated the gesture. "Live Long and Prosper."

Jalen grinned at him, shooting a quick glance at her

to see if she was getting all this coolness. Lia smiled back and finally decided to take mercy on Thomas before his poor overwhelmed brain exploded.

"Okay, Yaxley Yakkums," she said to Jalen. "Time to go."

Thomas raised one brow. *"Yaxley Yakkums?"*

"What else do you call a kid who never stops yakking?" she asked him.

"Indeed," Thomas murmured, a corner of his mouth twitching with a repressed smile.

Jalen apparently wasn't ready. "Aw, come on, man," he told her. "We're talking here."

"Sorry, *man.*" Lia got up and pulled Jalen to his feet. "But Thomas and I both need to get some work done today. So let's skedaddle. You'll see him again soon."

Jalen latched onto that last part like a crocodile trying to take down a water buffalo. "When? Can he come to dinner tonight? What about that, Mom? Why don't you cook dinner? I can help!"

Put squarely on the spot, Lia floundered, especially when she caught the amused glint in Thomas's eye. *Who's squirming now?* he seemed to ask. Lia hemmed and hawed for a minute, trying to decide what to do.

On the one hand, who was she to keep her son from his newfound father?

On the other hand, last-minute dinners were hard to pull off on a weekday. And why did she have to be cast in the role of bad guy?

On her second other hand, her prickling skin and hot cheeks told her that spending too much time with Thomas was a dangerous idea for her, personally. She'd been too long without a man in her life, and God knew he was the finest specimen she'd ever laid eyes on and, worse, the most intriguing.

Bottom line? Tonight was a bad idea, and she wasn't ready.

"Oh, I think we should try to do it another time—" she started.

"I'd love to," Thomas announced brightly, making it a point to ignore her warning glare. "What time should I come?"

"Awe-some!" Jalen did a triumphant fist pump.

And there it was already, Lia thought sourly. All her hard-won parental authority, usurped by the first father figure who happened along. Didn't take long.

"Jay, why don't you go back to Mrs. Brennan," she suggested, hoping to nip this whole dinner thing in the bud. "See if she can feed you another thousand calories' worth of candy while I talk to your...to Thomas."

"Okay!" The soul of cooperation now that he'd gotten his way, Jalen bounced out of the office, shutting the door behind him. "See you later!"

Looking shell-shocked, Thomas whooshed out a breath and shook his head in amazement. "I'm exhausted. I'd rather operate for thirty-six hours straight than go through that again."

"No kidding. I think it went well, though."

"Is he always like that?"

"Like what?" Lia asked, thinking he was referring to the nonstop talking.

"Intuitive. Curious. Self-assured. Strong."

Oh, man. It was a major thrill to see that Thomas was beginning to appreciate their son for the amazing kid he was. She smiled, her opinion of Thomas spiking another eighty-percent, easy.

"Yeah," she told him. "He's always like that."

He pressed his lips together, clearly struggling with unruly emotions and trying to find the right words. "I can see why you'd walk through fire for him."

"You can?"

"Yes."

She started to go, paused and then decided to press her luck. "Does that mean you forgive me? For turning your life upside down, I mean?"

"There's nothing to forgive, so let's forget that whole conversation. I didn't mean that, anyway. You know I didn't mean it." He hesitated. "You've done a great job with him."

The compliment was the last thing she'd expected to hear, especially from this stern taskmaster, and it messed with her brain, as did his absolution and how much it meant to her. She shrugged, trying to minimize both her accomplishments and her discomfort. Why did this man have such a gift for making her unravel?

"I haven't—"

"Yes." Unsmiling, he held her gaze. "You have."

The air did that slow sizzle around them, making her skin tingle and her blood heat. Since the last thing she needed was another awkward moment spent lusting after Dr. Sexy, she busied herself with one of the umpteen crises they had on hand. "Well. We didn't even get to the donor issue with Jalen. I guess that's a conversation for another day, huh?"

"Why can't we tell him tonight?"

"Tonight?"

"When I come for dinner."

"Oh." When he stared at her like that, with such utter focus, as though her face held all the secrets to the universe, she had a tough time stringing syllables together into a functional sentence. "You're not going to let me off the hook on that, are you?"

A smile worked at one corner of his mouth. "No. But I can bring Chinese or pizza or something. I don't expect you to cook for me."

Though she'd walk naked through a fire-ant mound before admitting it, she wanted to cook for him. She looked forward to showing off her skills a little. She loved to cook and bake and did it whenever she could manage, mostly because it helped her unwind and because cooking was one tiny thing she could do for Jalen that made his life seem more normal.

"Oh, don't bother," she said grudgingly. "I'll throw something together."

"Thanks," he said, his eyes bright with something that looked suspiciously like amusement. "Seven o'clock?"

"Fine. Don't be late."

"Oh, I won't."

There was a new note in his voice now, something husky, and it was way past time for her to go. Hurrying to the door, she put her hand on the knob and was milliseconds from a clean escape when he stopped her.

"Lia."

Cowardice took over, preventing her from glancing over her shoulder at him. The best she could do was stare at the door and wait. This, naturally, wasn't good enough for him.

"Look at me."

Giving herself a mental shake to get rid of these shivering nerves, she turned, and he came closer, and suddenly there wasn't nearly enough space between them. It was another beat or so before she could force herself to look up into his face.

That brown gaze of his had intensified and was now white hot. "Are you feeling this?"

Lia wanted to tell him not to look at her like that. Maybe they both needed a reminder of what she was—and what she wasn't. Her identity was tied up in being a widow, FBI analyst and, most importantly, single mother to a desperately ill child. Period. She wasn't a woman; she was a mom. There was no room in her life for an intriguing man who stopped her breath in its tracks, even if he was her son's father.

That being the case, she did the only logical thing: she lied.

"I don't know what you're talking about."

Thomas shuttered those amazing eyes and nodded as though he completely got it. He was barking up the wrong tree. Message received. No problemo.

Lia's breath eased with relief, even if she did feel a fleeting stab of disappointment in the region of her heart. Thank God he wasn't pressing the issue.

Without warning, Thomas reached out and grabbed her. She'd never been grabbed before; Alan had been way too respectful for that. Thomas wasn't, or maybe it was just that his urgency made him impatient.

Whatever.

The next thing she knew, he'd planted his hands on her intimate curves where waist met hips and was pulling her inside the hard, warm, thrilling circle of his arms, ignoring her sharp gasp of surprise. And then he was speaking low in her ear, and the electric brush of his lips against her sensitive skin was an excruciating pleasure that nearly sent her through the ceiling.

"This," he murmured. "The way I think about you when you're not here. The way I see your face. The way I want to put my hands all over you and swallow you whole. Are you feeling any of that for me? Are you feeling *this?"*

This was no time for lies. Not when he was whispering hot words to her and holding her as though he'd already had her. Not when her body was waking up after years in an unresponsive coma. Not when she wanted to ease him between her thighs and keep him there.

"Yes," she admitted. "Yes."

Against her cheek, she felt the shudder of his relieved breath.

"What are we going to do about it, Lia?"

Do? Was he for real? And had she lost her shaky grip on sanity to even be thinking of a way to get something started between them?

Pulling free of his possessive arms, she reached out and embraced her life partner: anger.

Anger because her kid was sick and her life was hard. Anger because she'd just given this man a tool to use against her in his relentless quest for sex, which was what all men wanted and the only thing most of them wanted. Anger, most of all, because he scared her to death and she hated being scared, and she hated him for showing her this glimmer of a passion that she could never indulge.

"Don't we have enough on our plates right now?" she demanded. "I'm focused on being the best mother I can to my sick son. I don't have room in my life for anything else. Not one more thing."

Thomas tensed and turned his head, refusing to meet her gaze while a vivid flush climbed his cheeks and a muscle ticked in his jaw. Frustration radiated off him in waves.

His silence did not make her feel better.

Still humming with anger and adrenaline, she stalked out, slamming the door behind her.

Okay, Thomas thought, rounding the corner of the E.R. nurse's station late that afternoon. He needed to do one last consult, take a quick shower and then head to Lia's. If he had no more interruptions, he'd have time to pick up a bottle of wine to thank her for having him to dinner. Or would flowers be better? All women liked flowers, but maybe she'd prefer the wine. On the other hand, did she even drink? He checked his watch, anticipation spiking in his blood. The main thing was not to be late, not that there was any real chance of that given how anxious he was to see both of them again. So... wine or flowers? Maybe chocolates would be good. There was a Godiva store—

"Earth to Thomas," said an amused voice. "Come in, Thomas. This is Tower, do you read me?"

Another voice chimed in, making that garbled static noise people used when they pretended to talk on a CB radio. "We're having some problems with reception, Tower. We seem to have lost all communication with

Thomas. Requesting permission to change course and intercept."

"Permission granted. Shoot that bastard down if you need to. We don't want to endanger the civilian population."

Ah, damn, Thomas thought. Just the distraction he didn't need if he wanted to get out of here on time.

He glanced over his shoulder without breaking stride, hoping to look busy enough that they'd leave him alone, and found himself face-to-face with Lucien and Jerome, whose cupped, static-making hand partially hid a wicked grin.

"Don't you two clowns have any lives to save this afternoon?" Thomas muttered as they fell in step on either side of him.

"Nope," Jerome said cheerfully. "Saved them all this morning."

Lucien, meanwhile, waved a dismissive hand. "I'm sick of saving lives. I think I'll do something more meaningful for a while. Maybe go to business school."

Even Thomas had to snort back a laugh at that unlikely image. "So? What's cooking down here? Anything interesting? Ebola? West Nile? Maybe an outbreak of syphilis? Talk to me."

"I got nothing," Lucien said.

"Guess who's hooking up with our intrepid chief of staff in the second-floor staff lounge?" Jerome asked.

Not more Germaine Dudley gossip again, Thomas thought, faking a loud and disinterested yawn. That man did more hooking up than a class of horny college freshmen. "We don't need to hear anything else about your mother's exploits, Jay."

"Wrong," Jerome said. "Not my mother. Kayla Tsang."

Thomas and Lucien stopped dead to stare at him. Lucien recovered first. "Kayla Tsang. 'Miss Thang.' Head nurse and a woman so cold that there's a layer of permafrost on her skin. No freaking way."

"Way," Jerome assured him. "I saw it with my own two eyes."

"And you weren't instantly blinded?" Thomas wondered, shuddering.

"Apparently not. Just thought you fellas would like to know that your boss is not *quite* as squeaky-clean as you might have thought. Oh, and there's no Santa Claus, either. Sorry to burst your bubbles."

Lucien stared at Thomas. "There's no Santa, man. What will we believe in now?"

Thomas clapped a reassuring hand on his shoulder. "There's always the Easter Bunny."

"True," Lucien said.

Jerome chuckled, pulled his buzzing phone out of his pocket and checked the display. "Oops. Patient's waking up down the hall. Gotta go," he said, speeding off around the corner.

"Me, too," Thomas told Lucien. "I'll check you later."

Lucien frowned and glanced at his watch. "Where're you going?"

"Well, if it was any of your business, I'd tell you that I'm leaving because I have a life."

"No, you don't."

"I do now," Thomas said before he could think to stop himself.

Lucien's eagle eyes sharpened, honing in on his face. "What's this? What's her name?"

Thomas thought of Lia and felt the slow burn in his cheeks. Then he thought of his son and felt the swell of emotion in his chest. But he wasn't ready to talk about either of them, not even with Lucien. Not yet. Everything was still too raw, too new.

"Again," he said, deciding to steer the conversation back onto a safer track, "none of your business. How do you like Dudley hooking up with Tsang after he gave you so much shit when you and Jasmine first got together?"

Lucien had fallen in love with his fiancée back when he was chief resident and she was his intern, thereby running afoul of the hospital's strict but unrealistic no-fraternization policy. Now he scowled. "I don't like it. It's a stupid rule, and that brother is the biggest hypocrite we've got going. And I'll tell you something else."

"I can hardly wait," Thomas said, checking his watch again with rising impatience. Now was not the time to tap into the flourishing hospital grapevine. Not when Lia and Jalen were expecting him soon.

"A couple of the other interns are playing footsie, or soon will be—Victor Aguilar and Tamara St. John."

Thomas gave in to a passing curiosity. "Those two? They fight like cats in a bag."

Lucien gave him a significant look. "You heard it here first."

Thomas had to grin as he broke away and headed off down the hall. "I feel sorry for you, my brother. I thought you had a life now. Thought you were too busy to be all up in everyone else's business. Jasmine must not be doing her job."

Lucien grinned and flushed like the lovesick idiot he was. "Oh, I have a life. Don't you worry none. Where're you going, though? That's what I want to know."

The answer was right on the tip of Thomas's tongue, so jarring and unexpected that he felt like he'd looked at the ends of his arms and discovered flippers instead of hands:

I also have a life outside the hospital, and I can't get to it fast enough.

Chapter 6

"He's here!" Jalen thundered down the stairs and slid through the foyer to the door, his voice echoing like a sonic boom in surround sound. Going to work on the dead bolt, he kept up his narrative commentary, as though there was some small chance that she hadn't heard him the first hundred and fifty times he screamed that Thomas had arrived. "He's here! Mom! He's here!"

She tried to smile, but wound up straining a cheek muscle with the effort. "I get it," she muttered, drinking deep from her second glass of Chianti and wondering when the wine would do its job and take the edge off her overwrought nerves. "He's here."

She'd seen Thomas arrive, of course, because she'd been peering out the kitchen window looking for him, all but holding her breath with anticipation. This, after dashing home from work, showering, carefully reapplying her minimal makeup and saying a fervent prayer of thanks that she knew what to do with a pork roast and a pressure cooker.

Then she'd made a salad, mashed some potatoes and cracked open a bottle of wine thinking she'd let it breathe. Usually, she didn't drink much, but some sort of self-medication seemed indicated if she wanted even a hope of relaxing and acting normally in Thomas's presence.

Half a bottle later, the wine was still breathing, and she was still hopped up on nerves thanks to Dr. McSexy and his sleek black BMW sedan, both of which were pulling into her driveway and parking behind her seven-year-old Camry this very second.

Standing behind the kitchen counter, where it felt safer, she watched as Jalen flung open the door and started yakking a mile a minute before poor Thomas could even make it over the threshold.

"Hi. You're right on time. Well, one minute late. I checked my watch. It's digital. See? Because I don't know how to read the ones with the face very well yet. We're having pork roast. With mashed potatoes. You're not a vegetarian, are you? Because you'll be hungry if you are, but Mom could probably fix you a PB&J so you can get some protein. Mom? He's here!"

"Hey, buddy." Thomas, grinning broadly and carrying a large shopping bag, came inside. "Thanks for having me."

He'd changed out of his doctor's uniform and now wore a black linen tunic, dark jeans and loafers that probably cost more than her monthly mortgage payment. The casual clothes, in theory, should have made him seem less overwhelming than when he'd sported the all-powerful scrubs-and-lab-coat combination, but no. If anything, his outfit emphasized another, equally dangerous aspect of him: his sexy, boyish side.

Oh, damn.

Lia drank again, draining her goblet dry and wishing she could gulp directly from the bottle for the rest of the evening. Might be easier.

"Thanks for coming," said Jalen, ever the gracious host. "What's in the bag?"

"Well, it's— Oh, shit! What's that?" Thomas cried, stumbling across the floor.

Bones, who liked to sleep in front of the French doors to the patio, the better to catch the afternoon sun, had woken, stretched, hopped over to inspect their new visitor and was now sniffing around Thomas's dancing feet. Having never been told that he was not, in fact, a German shepherd, he'd appointed himself the family's guardian and took this job very seriously. He was not fond of other males besides Jalen, and liked to show newcomers who the alpha rabbit was around there.

Which was probably why he bit a hole in the toe of Thomas's right shoe.

"Hey," Thomas cried, trying to shake free without kicking the bunny. "What the hell?"

"Oh, no," said Lia, already in motion.

Jalen got there first, scooping the animal up into a football hold. "This is Bones. Bones McCoy. And you should probably stop swearing because you're being a bad influence on me."

Thomas, looking beleaguered and bewildered,

looked across to Lia, who shrugged. "You wanted to come to dinner," she reminded him.

"Yeah, well, I didn't know I needed to sign a release first. A floppy-eared bunny? What's wrong with a goldfish?"

"A goldfish couldn't wear a pet-cam," Jalen supplied helpfully, pointing out Bones's collar. "Look."

Thomas leaned in closer for a better look, making sure to stay out of biting range. "Pet-cam. Cool. You get any good stuff with that?"

"Yeah. I'll get Mom's laptop and show you. BRB! That stands for *be right back!*"

He dashed off.

Thomas and Lia exchanged a bemused glance.

"I thought he was sick," Thomas said.

"He's still a kid. And he's excited that you're here."

"Hmm." Thomas made a show of looking all around the floor and under the coffee table. "Are there any other—"

"Mammals on the loose? No."

"So, it's safe for me to…"

She had to laugh. "Feel free to come closer."

Interest flared in his eyes. "How close?"

Laughing again, she shook her head and hoped her face wasn't as Day-Glo bright as it felt. "Not that close."

"Oh." Crossing to the counter, he set the bag on it and eyeballed her empty glass. "What're you drinking? Doesn't matter. I'll have a double."

"Sure thing," she said, reaching for a fresh goblet. What've you got there? Do you travel with your own dinner, or what?"

"No. I, ah, brought you something. To thank you for inviting me."

"I didn't invite you," she reminded him.

"Well, I'm polite."

Against all odds, Lia found herself loosening up, just a little, as though she might actually enjoy herself tonight without jumping out of her skin. Was that progress? Or the road to disaster? As she smiled into his smiling face, it didn't seem to matter so much. Not right now, anyway.

"So, what did you bring me?" she asked, pouring wine into both glasses.

"Nothing much. Just, you know—" he rummaged in the bag and pulled out a bottle "—some wine."

She took it; it was a nice pinot noir. "Wonderful. Thanks!"

Apparently he wasn't finished because a gold box from Godiva appeared. "And some chocolate."

"Oh, man. I love truffles. Thank you."

"And some, uh, flowers."

To her amazement, he reached into that bag and pulled out the most beautiful fishbowl of blazing red roses that she'd ever seen. How he'd managed to get it inside without spilling the water all over was a mystery.

"Oh, Thomas. Thank you," she breathed, trying not to simper like a fool.

He ducked his head and rubbed the back of his neck, looking embarrassed. Which made her wonder—could the great and arrogant doctor be as nervous as she was?

"It's no big deal."

"You know," she told him, her heart softening in

ways she didn't want to think about, "you don't need to spend a hundred dollars on gifts to thank someone for dinner."

He shrugged. "I'm a classic type-A over-achiever. You should probably know that about me."

"Is that right?" She laughed. "Is there anything else I should know about you?"

"Yeah," he said softly, unsmiling. "I've been looking forward to this all day."

His sudden vulnerability disarmed her. Thrilled her. Touched her.

"Well, then." Handing a glass to him, she raised her own in a toast. "To dinner with new friends."

"Friends?" he asked sourly.

"Take it or leave it," she warned.

"I'm taking it. I'm taking it."

The concession didn't fool her. The banked heat in his eyes told her he wasn't planning on settling for friendship from her—not by a long shot. Nor was she lured into any false sense of security because he'd let her escape from his office this afternoon without pursuing the subject of their raging attraction to each other. All they'd done, she knew, was postpone the looming moment of truth.

"Cheers," he said, raising his glass to hers.

She hesitated because any contact whatsoever between them was pregnant with meaning, and there seemed to be no way around it. Then, their gazes still locked together, she touched her glass to his with a tiny *clink*.

"Cheers."

* * *

"You doing okay, buddy?" Thomas asked after dinner.

"Yeah," Jalen said around a head-splitting yawn. Having showered and changed into a pair of green Starfleet Academy pajamas, the boy was now ready for bed and could barely keep his eyes open. Still, he settled next to Thomas on the sofa, curled his legs beneath him and unfolded a piece of notebook paper. "I'm not tired or anything."

Thomas, who was feeling a little drowsy himself but reluctant for this wonderful night to end and therefore knew where the kid was coming from, stifled a grin. Lia had turned out to be a spectacular cook, which didn't surprise him at all. Her delicious dinner and the wine and general coziness of this Cape Cod house, with its arched doorways, gleaming hardwood floors and tiny kitchen, relaxed him more than anything had since the day he set foot in medical school. Already, he'd begun to dread the return to his own house, which was four times the size of this one and half as welcoming.

The furniture here, for example, was weathered and comfortable, with pillows and ottomans, unlike the high-end, modern leather torture devices he had back home. The air here was fragrant with pork roast and some flickering floral candle Lia kept on the kitchen counter, but the air at his house was stale, except for Wednesdays, when the housekeeper left behind the smell of cleaning products. Most of all, this house had heart, with love and laughter and a crazy cat-size bunny to keep things interesting.

His house had only emptiness, even when he was home.

Hell, especially when he was home.

Which was probably why he never spent more than a few hours at a time there, if he could help it. The funny thing was, he'd never noticed how sad his beautiful house was.

Until now.

Yeah. He could stay right here for a lot longer than a couple of hours.

Lia, on the other hand, was still strung higher and tighter than a high-rise window washer, and she probably wanted to kick him out on his ass the first chance she got. She was hovering on the periphery, keeping a close eye on the proceedings while she shuttled dirty dishes from the dining room table back to the kitchen. If he had to guess, he'd say it was busywork to keep her from spending time with him.

Interesting.

Every now and then, he'd catch her watching him with unreadable eyes, and that gave him reason to hope. What he was hoping for, exactly, he had no idea. Well, he had some idea. A large part of it involved the two of them naked, twined around each other while rolling around on a horizontal surface. A large part of it didn't, though, and that was the troubling thing. He and women were all about sex. He didn't do other stuff, like meeting families, spending holidays together or restructuring his lifestyle to accommodate a partner.

So what was the thing about Lia? Why was she so... fascinating? She had a kid and a mortgage and wasn't the booty-call type at all. Plus, this temptation to get involved with the mother of his sick son wasn't the brightest idea he'd ever had. Like she'd said earlier, weren't things complicated enough? Why stir the pot? Hell, it would be easier to adopt triplets from Afghanistan than to have a disastrous affair with Lia and then try to co-parent with her. That being the case, he really needed to get a handle on his growing interest in her.

Only he didn't think he could.

"Jalen," she said now. "It's almost bedtime. You know that, right?"

"No way," Jalen complained.

"Way. And Thomas needs to get home soon, anyway. Isn't that right, Thomas?"

"Ah," Thomas began, distracted by that hopping menace of a glorified rat, who was now snuffling around the bottom of the sofa, probably planning his next assault.

"So wrap it up, okay?" Lia said.

Jalen groaned. "But—"

"You heard your mother." Thomas tried a stern parental voice on for size and discovered that he had one and that Jalen seemed to respond to it.

"Okay," Jalen grumbled darkly, showing every sign of docility. "Can we just look at my list first?"

"Well, ah…" Lia seemed startled by this sudden cooperation. Her gaze, vaguely suspicious, swung between the males and settled on Thomas, even as she spoke to the boy. "Sure." After a hesitation, she opened and closed her mouth a couple of times, clearly undergoing some sort of painful struggle with herself.

Thomas waited, his heart thumping.

Thank you, she mouthed.

Because it wouldn't be cool to jump up and do a joyous fist pump, Thomas just winked. Ducking her head and looking flustered, Lia went back to the dishes, clanking several of the plates together as she stacked them.

"I'll get those," he told her. "Least I can do."

"But—"

"Have some more wine." His tone was inching toward dictatorial, and she raised her brows accordingly. *Not good, Bradshaw. The pretty lady won't unwind enough to have a conversation with you if you bark orders at her.* "Please."

"You're a bad influence, Doctor," she said, reaching for the bottle.

"I try." With difficulty, he peeled his gaze away from Lia and discovered, with a start, that Jalen was studying him with those keen eyes of his. "What're you staring at, Shorty?"

"You like my mom, don't you?"

Damn. Was anything about being with a kid easy?

"Well, yeah," Thomas stammered. "Of course I like her."

Jalen rolled his eyes. "No. I mean you *like* her."

From over in the kitchen came the sound of a utensil clattering to the floor, but Thomas didn't dare risk a glance at Lia now lest he do something truly goofy, like blush or grin.

Maybe he should try the parental thing again. Maybe frown or something. Body language was important with kids, right? There. He did it.

"That's a grown-up topic, youngling. And I'm not sure it's any of your business."

Jalen snorted with clear disbelief. "Of course it's my

business. She's my mom! Just don't go kissing her in front of me or anything, okay? I can't deal with that."

Kissing.

Funny the boy should mention it, because he had, in fact, spent a generous portion of the evening wanting to kiss Lia and wondering whether she'd let him. This train of thought was clearly at odds with his whole don't-stir-the-pot strategy, but the more Lia inched her way under his skin, the less he cared. The one thing he knew for sure was that if—no, when—he kissed Lia, he damn sure didn't want an audience.

"You got it, buddy." Thomas glanced back to the kitchen, where Lia was standing, still as marble, and held her gaze. "I won't kiss her in front of you."

A frozen beat or two passed, and then Lia turned away, gulping from her goblet.

Oh, yeah, Thomas thought. This one was a special combination of warrior woman and vulnerable rose. He did indeed like her. A lot.

"Okay, so here's my list."

Get your head back in the game, Bradshaw.

Thomas gave his head a quick shake and looked down at his son. "List? What list?"

"I made a list of dad things you should do. Things I expect you to do. Because things go smoother when you talk about what you expect. They taught us that in school. So, here goes."

Jalen cleared his throat and edged closer, into the crook of Thomas's arm where it rested across the back of the sofa. Thomas marveled again at the kid's weight. His wiry strength and warmth. The scent of his musky

Old Spice–type body wash, which he'd apparently saturated himself with during his shower.

Kids were a miracle. This kid was a miracle.

Was it okay to touch him? To give in to this primal paternal urge and snuggle a little? Wasn't that what fathers and sons did at bedtime? That paralyzing awkwardness hit him again, and he floundered, desperate not to do the wrong thing and screw things up. He thought of what the Admiral would have done with him and decided that, from now on, that would be his guidepost: decide what the Admiral would do in the same situation and then do the opposite.

So he put his arm around Jalen and scooped him closer, right up against his side. And then, because the kid didn't kick up a protest, he leaned down to kiss his soft temple.

Man, it felt good. It felt really, really good.

"Number one," Jalen read. "No spankings."

Thomas thought back to the Admiral's discipline, which had consisted of liberal amounts of corporal punishment with hands, belts, wooden spoons and anything else the Admiral could grab in the heat of frustration or anger. He shuddered at the memories.

"You got it. No spankings."

Jalen grinned with relief. "Number two, you have to call me at bedtime."

This made Thomas frown. Not because it would be a pain in the ass to call every night, but because it hit him for the first time that Jalen lived here and he lived somewhere else, and even if they worked up a schedule where Jalen spent weekends or some such with him, there'd be plenty of bedtimes that he'd miss.

The idea didn't sit right with him. It made his chest hurt. He frowned again, deeper.

Jalen noticed, of course. He seemed to decide that the request was unreasonable and began to backpedal. "You don't have to call *every* every night."

"Yes, I do." Thomas pressed another kiss to his forehead and hugged his thin shoulders. "I'm happy to call you every night. What else?"

Another delighted grin from Jalen, which felt like a winning lotto number to Thomas.

"Number three, I'm going to call you Thomas for now. Because *Daddy* feels a little weird since we just met. Don't you think?"

No, he didn't think. He didn't like. But since he was following the boy's cues and going at his speed rather than his own, he faked it. "You got it."

"Number four, my birthday's in a few weeks. Don't forget."

"Got it."

"Excellent." Jalen refolded the list with clear satisfaction. "That's it."

"Wait, that's it? You don't want to ask for a pony or a big-screen TV for your room or anything?"

"Nope."

Amazement made Thomas's jaw drop open in a gape. "What kind of kid are you?"

"The best," Jalen said simply. "Can you tuck me in?"

"Yeah." Thomas blinked and swallowed, trying not to choke on all this scary emotion, while Lia, still watching from the kitchen, gave him a slow smile full of understanding. "I can do that."

Chapter 7

When Thomas came down the stairs ten minutes later, he looked different, Lia thought. His steps were slower, his face grimmer and more thoughtful. Even those broad shoulders of his had a slight droop.

Lia, who'd been in the middle of bagging up the leftover salad, started to ask him what was wrong, but that seemed pointless. Maybe he'd seen the drugstore-worthy array of medications sitting on Jalen's dresser or caught a glimpse of the clipboard next to his bed, on which she recorded his miscellaneous symptoms and treatments, or seen the wall full of handmade get-well cards from his classmates at school. Or maybe it was just the enormity of all the recent changes in his life, catching up with him at last.

Whatever it was, Thomas looked shell-shocked. Forever altered.

The nurturer in her—and as a mother, she was mostly nurturer, wasn't she?—wouldn't let her pretend she didn't see what was going on. That felt too unnatural, like trying to sleep while standing up. So instead, she offered him the most basic level of support. Support 101. How much trouble could that get her into?

"Hey," she said. "You okay?"

He frowned, his brows lowering with irritated embarrassment as he came into the kitchen and reached for the sponge. "Of course. Why wouldn't I be?"

Ah. Of course. The coolheaded surgeon would never allow himself to be shaken by his own sick kid. Or the fact that he even had a kid. Uh-uh. Not him. Never show emotion. That was probably the first thing they told you in medical school, right after they gave you your first stethoscope.

She could almost laugh at his calm, cool and collected act, but she'd spent too much time in that same dark place, just struggling to be strong and keep it together for one more day.

So she waited, dying to see if he could pull it off.

He couldn't. He stared, unfocused, at the sponge in his hand for several long beats and might have stared forever, but Lia had seen enough.

She reached out, rubbing a hand over his shoulder. "It's okay."

That did it. Thomas's face twisted, and he bent double at the waist, dropping the sponge into the sink and hanging on to the counter for support.

"I need a minute," he said, shoulders heaving. "I just need—"

Breaking off, he straightened and paced away, head

pressed between his hands. Lia studied her shoes and gave him time. After a couple of laps around the tiny kitchen, the fearsome Dr. Bradshaw was back and firmly in charge. Snatching up the sponge again, he plunged his arms into the soapy water and attacked the dishes.

"What was he like as a baby?"

Lia had to laugh. "Colicky. He loved rice cereal. Hated peaches. Potty-trained at eighteen months because he didn't like to lie still long enough for me to change his diapers."

"What was his first word?"

Lia laughed again, thinking of all those late night feedings, just her and Jalen with the TV. "*Spock.* Because I used to watch reruns when I was breast-feeding him."

Thomas grinned, those boyish dimples grooving up his cheeks as he laughed. "*Spock.* Should have been *Mama.*"

"I know, right?"

"When did he start reading?"

Lia took a dish from the rack to rinse and dry. "He was four. In his second year of preschool. *Where the Wild Things Are.* I think he finally just memorized all the pages."

"*Where the Wild Things Are.* Good choice. I would have gone for *The Cat in the Hat*, but *Wild Things* is a respectable choice."

"I'm so glad you think so. I live for your approval."

The grin was still on her lips when she reached into the soapy water for the lone remaining glass, forgetting that his hand was already in there. By the time her stuttering heart reminded her, it was already too late. His fingers were gliding over the back of her hand, twining their fingers together in a grip that felt as strong and unbreakable as a sequoia. The only thing she could do was hold tight and flick her gaze up to meet his.

They were too close. His unsmiling face was everything in her field of vision, and his stunning brown eyes were overwhelming. They were flecked with gold and green, so expressive with their fears and desires that it seemed unlikely she'd ever get bored with staring into them. His skin was smooth, his jaws sleek, his lips curved and sensual.

And, standing here with him, she was in worse trouble than she'd ever dreamed.

"I didn't expect my life to change this fast," he told her, his wet thumb smoothing over the back of her hand in slow circles.

Yeah. She knew the feeling. "Kids can do that to you."

He blinked, letting her hand go and looking for the towel. "Yeah. Kids."

Sudden awkwardness reached out to smother her. In the oppressive silence, she didn't know what to do with her hands or where her feet wanted to walk her, so she stood there, probably looking goofy. She watched Thomas dry his hands and then followed him to the living room, where he paused to look at one of the framed photos sitting on the coffee table—this one of Alan in the driveway, waxing his classic Mustang, the one he'd been killed in.

Thomas picked it up to study it more closely and she watched the darkening frown as it spread over his face, overcome by a feeling of disorientation. She felt, suddenly, as though she was cheating on Alan, and yet with Thomas here, so vibrantly masculine and intense, she had a hard time conjuring up anything about Alan except for that one-dimensional image of his smiling face. His voice? His laugh? His scent? All disconnected and vague memories growing fainter the more time she spent with Thomas.

This wasn't right.

Without a word, she took the photo out of his hands and replaced it on the coffee table, where it belonged. She did not look at it as she did so.

"You loved him," he said softly.

"Yes."

"Tell me about him."

How could she explain anything when Alan was slipping further away by the second? Should she try to explain her desolation when he died? Her stark fear about raising a child by herself? Or how about her slow return to life along with the dawning discovery that she was strong and could stand on her own two feet? What about the first time she didn't cry herself to sleep, or the first time she laughed freely, without guilt?

What about now, when she could barely remember the feeling of her husband's hands on her body because she was so hungry for Thomas's touch?

How could she explain that, even to herself?

"He worked in the U.S. Attorney's office. I met him when he was prosecuting this guy we'd grabbed for running a pyramid scheme on the internet. He was a widower. He had a wicked sense of humor. I loved him. We laughed a lot together, and then he died."

There it was. A life—their life together—summarized in ten sentences or less.

The bleakness of her loss was still there, but, she realized, at a manageable level.

The guilt was crushing.

"You still miss him." Thomas's voice was hollow.

She stared at Thomas. "Not as much."

A flair of understanding—and something hotter—lit in his eyes. "You feel guilty."

"Yes."

"You're still alive, Lia."

"Yes."

"Maybe you should live."

"You say that like it's easy."

"I'm sorry," he told her.

"For what?"

"Your life has been way too hard."

She shrugged, because what was there to say to that? It wasn't like she was the only woman out there who'd ever been widowed and tried to raise a child alone. "I'm still standing."

"You're amazing," he told her quietly, his expression rapt, and he didn't smile to mitigate the power of the words. "You absolutely blow my mind."

She started to say something, to deny it, but all she could produce was the sigh of his name. "Thomas."

He blinked and turned, hurrying for the door as though he regretted everything he'd just said and therefore couldn't leave fast enough. "I've got to go. We'll know if I'm a match or not in a few days."

"Right," she said helplessly, thrown off-kilter by the sudden change of topic. "A few days."

"And I'll want to see him again. Tomorrow, if we can work it out."

"Okay," she said, nodding like some stupid bobble-head doll.

They were at the door now, and he was almost gone. She'd held it together pretty well, she thought, except for the hand-holding thing, but that was no big deal in the scheme of things. The important thing was not to look into those eyes again.

"And I'm going to need that kiss now."

"What?"

His attention had zeroed in on her lips, and he looked utterly mesmerized. Using those surgeon's hands—those unspeakably talented and gentle surgeon's hands—he reached out to trace his thumbs over her mouth. He skimmed the bow of her top lip and the plump ridge of her bottom, crooning with approval, and she watched, enthralled, as his lids lowered and his face colored with excitement.

"You're beautiful," he said softly. "You know that?"

Since she didn't handle compliments well, the denial was automatic. "I'm not—"

"Shh." He drifted closer, touching only her mouth, and dipped his head, giving her time to get used to his approach, his physicality. "Haven't you had enough wine to get ready for this? What are you so afraid of?"

Somehow, when he was being this tender and his voice was such a soft caress, there was nothing to do but be honest and come out with it. "It's been so long for me," she confessed. "And it's the way you look at me."

His brow quirked with surprise. "How's that?"

"I can't describe it. It's like I'm being burned."

He stilled. Took a deep breath. Banked some of that overwhelming intensity.

"I'm not going to burn you." Sliding his hand lower, he tipped her chin up enough to receive his mouth. "You'll see."

"I thought we agreed that this was too much with everything else."

"No," he said. "I listened. I didn't agree. There's a difference."

"Then let's agree now."

"To what? You want me to pretend I can stop thinking about you? Well, I can't."

"Thomas—"

"We're smart people, aren't we? We can figure this out as we go."

With that, he closed the final distance, fitted his sweet, sweet lips to hers, and kissed her until the world spun. If she'd needed any proof that, just as she'd feared, her nose was wide-open where he was concerned, this was it. She couldn't lose herself in him fast enough. It was a slow, lingering kiss that gave more than it demanded, and she was just softening for him, humming with desire, ready to open her mouth, arms and legs to anything he wanted, when it was over and he was pulling back.

Breathless, she put a steadying hand on the doorknob and tried not to wobble. She had the unaccountable feeling that he'd just told her everything she needed to know, and she felt…reassured.

He stared at her, his gaze turbulent and unreadable. And then he left without a word.

* * *

Hang on. Was that the phone?

Groggy, Lia struggled her way free of the linens and sat up, giving her noggin a big thunk against the headboard in the process. It had been a restless night of sexual frustration interrupted by periods of extreme anxiety bordering on panic when she remembered kissing Thomas. What the hell had she been thinking? She cracked open her bleary eyes and checked the time on her digital clock: 5:52. In the morning. Turning on the lamp seemed like way too much torture this early, so she snatched up the bleating phone by the fourth obnoxious ring and hit the button.

"Hello?" she snarled without bothering to check the display. "This better be good because it's not even six freaking o'clock."

"Good morning, sunshine." Oh, God. It was Thomas. Thomas! Sounding bright and chipper, and here she was, acting like a banshee. "It is good. I hope you don't mind me calling like this. My day starts pretty early. Plus, I couldn't sleep last night. I was thinking about you, in case you want to know."

Her innate eloquence kicked in. "Oh," she said. "Umm…"

"The preliminary test results are in," he said, cutting across her stammering. "I called in about a thousand favors to get them expedited."

Her heart gave out, refusing to pump any more blood. "And?"

"I'm a match." He took a deep, shuddering breath. "I'm a match."

* * *

"Don't be scared." Lia hurried down the endless hallway, trying to look upbeat while staying out of the way of the swinging IV bags and keeping one eye on the looming double metal doors that would separate her from her son for the next three or four hours. She was putting him in the hands of the transplant team. And God, of course. She sent up a silent prayer, asking God to bless the team with cool heads, clear eyes and steady hands. Asking Him to keep her boy safe and bring him back to her. "There's nothing to be scared of, okay? They'll take good care of you."

Down on the wheeled bed, wrapped up in institutional white blankets topped with his navy fleece blanket from home, Jalen stared up at her with drowsy eyes. The sedative was beginning to take effect, but that did not prevent him from stealing a furtive glance at the orderlies on either side of the bed and then giving her a final look of extreme exasperation.

"Mo-om. I'm not…scared. Don't…embarrass me."

Of course. A kid had to protect his street cred at all costs. Even when he held his mother's hand in a death grip that threatened to cut off all circulation.

"Sorry," she told him. "I know you're not scared."

If he wasn't admitting it, then she couldn't admit it, either. Moms could never admit any weakness. She would, therefore, keep that reassuring smile plastered on her lips and ignore the clammy sweat trickling down her spine right this very second. She would not give way to the rising terror that burned her throat. She would not think thoughts such as:

What if the new kidney doesn't take?

What if there's some terrible complication?
What if he dies on the table?

No. She would keep her chin up and her shoulders squared. She would be strong.

For Jalen.

Those double doors were right there now, waiting to swallow up her son.

"Okay, Mom," said Janet, one of the nurses, with a kindly smile and a reassuring arm squeeze as they stopped the bed and paused. "Tell this boy you'll see him soon."

Oh, God.

Her smile quivered, but Lia thought she did a pretty good job of hanging on to it. She leaned over Jalen, imprinting every feature in her memory for the one-billionth time. The curl of his hair against his forehead. He needed a trim soon. The smoothness of his brown skin, the baby fat that clung to those plump cheeks, even now, and the quiet wisdom in those sleepy brown eyes.

"I'll see you soon, okay?" she murmured, kissing his temple.

"Don't cry, Mom."

"I'm not crying," she said, blinking furiously.

"I'm going to…be better soon."

"I know you are, baby."

"Mo-om. I'm not a baby."

His voice was fading, and his eyes were closing. She was losing him to the sedatives, but it was too soon, and there were things that she should say at a moment like this, things he needed to hear.

"I'm proud of you, Jalen."

"I…know," he said.

He did? Well, good. She told him often enough. "You behave, okay?"

"O-kay."

"See you soon."

With a final kiss and a nuzzle, she straightened and nodded at Janet, who gave her arm another squeeze. Someone punched the automatic-door button, and the doors whooshed open to reveal yet another inner world of this hospital, a place where mothers didn't belong and weren't allowed. They started moving again, wheeling the bed, and Lia started to step back.

Except that Jalen wouldn't let go of her hand.

She leaned down again and whispered in his ear. "What is it, Jay?"

"You didn't…say you…love me."

That emotion trapped in her throat squeezed tighter, forcing her to stifle a sudden sob. She would not cry… she would not cry…she would not—

"I thought you didn't want me to embarrass you," she reminded him.

Jalen never opened his eyes. "Yeah, but parents…are supposed to say they love their kids at a…at a…time like this."

Well, what could she do?

"I love you, Jay," she said, kissing that sweet forehead again. "I love you."

Chapter 8

The second Jalen disappeared from sight, Lia wheeled around and hurried back into the pre-op area, heading for Thomas's room. There was still time for her to see him before they took him down, and she wanted—

"Wait," she said, banging through the door into a room with a window, a chair and a tray table, but no bed and no Thomas. "Where's Thomas?"

An aide or orderly poked his head out of the bathroom, where he'd apparently been cleaning. "Gone. They took him about five minutes ago."

"Took him?" Bewildered and dangerously close to losing it, Lia checked her watch, looked back at the aide, checked her watch again and pointed to it, so this guy would be sure to get the picture. Maybe if she made this perfectly clear, Thomas would reappear, and she'd have time to wish him well and send him on his way before he sacrificed a body part to save their son. "It's not time yet. They weren't supposed to take him for ten more minutes. It's not time."

The aide held up both hands as though she'd waved a gun during a stickup. "I didn't have nothing to do with it. All I know is that they came and—"

"It wasn't time," she shrieked.

The man, a senior with flecks of gray in his hair and understanding eyes, gave her a reassuring wink. "Don't you worry none. They'll take good care of him, you hear?"

Mute with paralysis, she nodded.

The man left, taking his cleaning cart with him, and Lia sank into the lone chair.

The shakes overtook her, wracking her body, as though she'd just finished an arctic trek and lost all her body heat. Resting her elbows on her knees, she clasped her hands together and rocked back and forth, aiming for a self-comfort that stubbornly refused to come.

All she could think of was the things she hadn't had the time—or the chance—to tell Thomas. The two days since the test results came back had passed in a whirl of tests and scheduling and last-minute details involving releases and insurance and God-knew-what that she couldn't even remember. Now the opportunity was lost, and Thomas had gone into that O.R. all alone, without anyone to hold his hand and wish him well. And there were risks for him in there; they'd tried not to talk about them, but they existed. What if Thomas had complications, and she hadn't even sent him off properly? What then?

Pain knifed through the center of her chest, threatening to cut her in two.

Had she thanked Thomas? Really *thanked* him?

Had she told him how brave and honorable she thought he was?

Had she told him that it was hard to breathe when he looked at her?

Would she ever have the chance to tell him, or had she wasted the only opportunity she'd ever get? Funny how her fears about romantic relationships and being vulnerable didn't amount to diddly-squat now that she had the time to worry about whether Thomas would come out of that procedure in one piece.

Working hard to keep the despair and fear at bay, Lia rocked herself a little harder and settled in for the long wait for both of the males in her life.

Thomas floated in the clouds, trying to slip back into the sweet white oblivion that hovered just out of reach. For reasons unknown, some idiot insisted on calling his name and trying to pull him back to solid earth, and he didn't like it any more than he liked the annoying beeping of some unseen machine.

"Thomas," said the voice again. "Come on, now."

Okay, wait. He recognized that voice. Liked that voice. It sounded like Lia.

Lia.

He slammed back into his body with a hard jolt, struggling against both the breathing tube stuck up his nose and his brain, which refused to come up to speed and seemed to have been replaced with cotton fluff.

"I knew you were going to be a lousy patient," said

Lia, reaching out to soothe him with her cool hands. "It's okay. It's okay."

This was no time for soothing, even if he did love it when she touched him. Jerking the cannula out of his nose, he forced his heavy lids open and tried to focus. Damn nurses had him wired up like the sound system at a Prince concert, with IV lines and tubes everywhere.

"Jalen," he croaked. "How's Jalen?"

Lia smiled, a beam of purest sunlight, and he knew right then, because he'd never seen her look so happy and his eyes had never seen anything so beautiful. Still, he needed to hear it.

"He's great," she said.

"Yeah?" he slumped back against the pillows—not that he'd have been able to go anywhere anyway—flattened by such blinding relief that the emotion overwhelmed him and his face crumpled. Embarrassed, he lifted his hand to cover his eyes and tried to get a grip.

"Yeah. The kidney took right away. It's functioning already, and everything looks great. He'll wake up soon, so I need to go, but I just wanted to say…thank you."

Thomas swiped at his eyes and met her gaze, trying to hold the anesthesia- and sedative-induced fogginess at bay for another minute.

"You're welcome."

"I'm sorry I didn't get to see you before they took you into surgery. I came by after they took Jalen, but you were gone already."

Renewed disappointment needled at him, not that he wanted to guilt-trip her or anything. Nor did he want her to know how much her absence had stung. He shrugged, trying to appear unconcerned. "It's okay."

"No, it's not." She stared down at him, her tired face aglow with admiration. "I think you're amazing. I just want you to know that."

This, to his surprise, annoyed him. "I'm not some big hero. I just did the right thing."

"That's why you are a hero."

Yeah, okay. Now she was starting to piss him off. What kind of a jerk did she think he was? That he'd let his son wait for a kidney from someone else, perhaps die, rather than give him one of his own?

And did she see nothing else worthwhile in him?

With a supreme act of will, he kept his heavy lids open and focused on her face. "We need to get past this gratitude thing. That's not what I want from you."

She stilled, seeming to hold her breath. "What do you want from me?"

"Everything else," he murmured, the drugs making him more open and honest than he'd meant to be this soon in their budding relationship. "Everything."

The last thing he saw before his eyes drifted closed was the soft and beautiful smile that curled her lips.

"Go to sleep, Thomas." That sweet mouth of hers pressed a lingering kiss to his forehead. "I'll see you later."

"Mom!" Jalen woke in a sudden flurry of arms and legs, flailing as though he'd been woven into a spider's web and needed to escape. "I don't like it! I don't like it!"

"It's okay, buddy." Lia, who'd been sitting in a chair right by the bed, quickly leaned in to hold his shoulders and settle him down before he yanked his IV line or tore his stitches or some such. "Open your eyes. You're fine."

"I don't like this," Jalen grumbled blearily, pulling the cannula out of his nose and over his head before she could stop him. He cracked open his eyes and blinked at her, his expression baleful even though his color was pink with newfound health. "And I'm thirsty."

"I think we can do something about that." There was a cup of ice water with a bent straw on the tray table for just such an occasion, and she raised the head of the bed a little and propped him up so he could sip. The anesthesia might make him a little nauseous, so they had to be careful about that. "Now drink slowly," she said.

Jalen latched onto the straw and drank in greedy slurps, nearly draining the cup before she had the presence of mind to snatch it away. "Hey!"

Satisfied, he slumped back against the pillows, his eyes closing again. She watched, heart swollen with joy, as he moved his arms under the blankets, running his hands over the bandages on his right side.

"So, do I have a new kidney now?"

"You do indeed."

"Is it working good?"

"It's working great."

"No more dialysis?"

"No more dialysis."

"Awesome." Eyes still closed, Jalen managed a drowsy grin. "Let's party."

"I'm in here," Thomas called.

Lia, who'd had to kick the front door shut because her arms were full of bags and bundles, did a sharp

U-turn away from the spiral staircase leading to the upper level of Thomas's house and veered into the living-room area. The newly sprung patient was sprawled across a sleek black leather sofa that looked as though it had been stolen from the Jetsons or some other space-age family. The place was really very cool, she thought, with floor-to-ceiling windows on three sides, exposed pipes and walkways, funky black-and-white paintings on the walls and, of course, a monstrous flat-screen TV mounted over the black marble fireplace.

She stared down at him, wondering how he planned to get comfortable when the lone pillow on the sofa—if you could call it a pillow—seemed to be a block of red foam with some black piping on it.

"You okay?"

"Never better," he said, arranging the pillow under his neck.

"Oh, really? Well, your *never better* looks a little pale and sickly to me."

He gave her a doleful look from beneath droopy eyelids. "Please do not insult my manhood."

Laughing, she set her bags on the floor because the sparkling glass coffee table didn't have a single speck of dust on it and she hated the thought of smudging it. "You're down one kidney, Doctor. Your body needs to adjust. I don't think it's a sign of dishonor if you admit to being a little tired."

"I do not admit to weakness."

"Great. Since you're doing so well, I'll just be on my way."

"On the other hand," he said, his voice noticeably

fainter and more pitiful than it had just been, "I am a little…off-kilter."

"Poor baby," she murmured.

"Someone probably should take care of me. Just in case I need anything."

"Well…" She hesitated. "If you think that's wise."

He nodded solemnly. "I do."

"Then it's a good thing I'm here, isn't it?"

"It's the best thing. For my health. You know."

"Anything for your health."

"Come here."

He stretched out a hand to her, and she took it, thinking that medical crises had a strange way of breaking down barriers and creating intimacy. In the last several days, she'd gotten way too used to touching him. Anticipating his needs. Smiling at him. So it didn't feel that odd when he shifted to make room for her to sit on the edge of the sofa at his hip and when he smoothed her hair behind her ear and then rubbed the strands between his thumb and forefingers as though he was testing the quality of a bolt of silk.

"Thanks for bringing me home," he told her.

Nerve endings tingled to life all up and down her scalp and neck. She shrugged, trying to disguise the involuntary shiver. "Oh, you know. When you donate a kidney, you get a ride home. It's a rule."

He grinned, displaying those fabulous dimples. "And if I donate blood?"

"Cab ride."

His husky laughter slid under her skin and inside her, making it harder to breathe.

"I think you like me a little bit, Lia," he told her,

those fingers moving up her neck and around back to her nape, where they kneaded and soothed.

She tried to focus on his face. Tried to swallow the slow croon that wanted to rise up out of her throat and give her away. Tried not to let her head fall back and her spine arch.

"There you go, getting cocky."

Another laugh, this one followed by a low murmur. "You don't like me? Just a little bit?"

Would it hurt anything if she closed her eyes and leaned back into his caress? Just this once? She was so tired. What could it hurt? "I will concede," she told him, "that there is a slight possibility—"

"Only slight?"

"—that you may not be, on closer examination, as big a jackass as I first thought you were. But that's not my final word on the subject, and it's all pending further developments."

"So I'm a small jackass? Is that it?"

Opening her eyes, she stared down into his, making a connection that was like freefalling through space. She took a deep breath and worked on regulating her thundering heartbeat before it made her ribs crack.

"You're not a jackass."

"No?"

"No."

"You sure?"

Sitting here with him like this, when they were both drowsy and his warm hands were so comforting and when he'd banked most of the intensity that usually burned in his eyes, replacing the arrogant surgeon with the boyish man who was as vulnerable as she was, it felt safe to tell him the truth. This once. "You're smart and funny. You're demanding, but I think you're harder on yourself than you are on anyone else. You're brave and strong and sexy—"

"And you like me."

"—and I like you."

"Good," he said, unsmiling. "Because I'm crazy about you. In case you hadn't noticed. So go easy on me, okay?"

"Okay," she said softly.

That seemed to satisfy him. Nodding, he let his eyes drift closed, but his hands went to her hips, anchoring her there beside him in case she had any plans to leave just yet. And she studied everything about him. His brown skin. The shadowy bristle of his beard, because he hadn't shaved in a couple of days. The sleek brows, the long lashes. The tender curve of his mouth. And she wanted—

"Did you bring something for me?"

Did she what? Oh, yeah. *Get back into the game, girl.*

Trying to return to business, she looked to her bags, reminding herself. "A blanket. Some magazines. Dinner for later."

"Chicken soup? Smells homemade."

"I'll have you know that this is creamy chicken soup with shiitake mushrooms and wild rice."

One edge of his mouth curved in a smile, but he didn't open his eyes. "You'll spoil me."

"You deserve it."

He sighed, settling deeper into the sofa.

Well, there was no time like the present to get the

soup into the fridge, she supposed, starting to stand. And while she was here she could check his supplies and make sure he had bread, milk and eggs and the like. God knew what a bachelor like him ate if left to his own devices. And she should—

"Stay with me."

Startled, she looked down to discover those eyes open again, focused and intent. She gestured helplessly to the bag, to the kitchen, trying to encompass all the things she needed to do, all the responsibilities and duties she had to manage.

"I can't," she began.

Wrong answer. His brows lowered, darkening his entire face. "I'm going to take care of you, whether you make it easy for me or not. I'm tired. You've been staying at the hospital with Jalen, so I know you're tired. We both need a nap. I've got a sofa and you brought a blanket." He opened his arms in the sweetest invitation she'd ever seen. "Stay with me. Please."

Part of her wanted to resist. A bigger part of her wanted nothing more than this, now, with him. So, after a slight hesitation, she grabbed the fleece blanket from its bag and stayed, stretching out alongside him on that big sofa, twining her legs with his and resting her cheek against the solid warmth of his chest. Lying with him was like entering a wonderful hybrid zone where heaven met home, and she knew right away that, after this, sleeping alone would always be a letdown.

But she would worry about that later.

With a murmur of approval, he shook the blanket

open and covered them both with it, kissed the top of her head and held her tight while she surrendered to the exhaustion.

Chapter 9

"Did you give Bones the carrots?" Jalen asked, his restless legs moving under the blanket and knocking over the pile of UNO cards that Lia had just painstakingly arranged and stacked. "You can't forget the carrots."

Lia, who had been sitting in the bedside chair, scrambled to catch the cards as they cascaded to the floor and wondered if anyone would call child protective services on her if she bopped the patient upside the head. The hospital room had, in the last couple of days, begun to feel like a prison cell for both of them—although, in fairness, she thought that she was suffering way more than Jalen was. They could not get out of here soon enough, as far as she was concerned. Jalen was restless, whiny and generally bored out of his mind, which translated to wall-to-wall misery for Lia, who'd been struggling to keep him both quiet and entertained.

Still, she tried to be mature and patient. She was, after all, the adult here.

"As I explained to you before," she said, recovering the cards and keeping most, but not all, of the edginess out of her voice, "I fed Bones before I left the house."

"Yeah, but did you give him the carrots or the celery?" Jalen, who was now the picture of glowing health, with pink cheeks, bright eyes and only the IV line in his arm to remind the world that he'd just had major surgery, did a little mini-flop against the pillows to highlight his apparent frustration at having to explain the whole rabbit diet thing to such a dolt. "He likes carrots in the morning and celery at dinner. And did you download the images from his bunny cam? When can I see them?"

Lia sighed. Yeah, she'd had nothing better to do this week than download the bunny-cam images of the undersides of all the furniture in her house.

Right on cue, there was a brisk knock on the door, and Thomas poked his head inside. "What's going on in here, people?"

"Thank you, Jesus," muttered Lia, even though she wasn't sure she was ready to face him again so soon after today's interlude on the sofa.

Jalen perked up, apparently thrilled to have someone else take up his fight. "Mom didn't feed Bones his carrots this morning," he complained. "I've got to get out of here and get back home before she kills him."

Thomas, wearing a black T-shirt, jeans and a baseball hat, and still moving a bit slower than usual, shot Lia a glance of wry amusement, as though he understood perfectly. "I'm pretty sure your mom will not kill Bones between now and tomorrow, when you go home."

"She might!"

"I'm going to kill someone," Lia murmured, and Thomas stifled a snort of laughter. "Maybe a couple of people. Why aren't you home resting, where I left you? Why can't you stay put?"

Thomas flapped a dismissive hand. "I'm not good at lying around."

"Now's your chance to practice."

"Absolutely," Thomas agreed brightly. "As soon as I look in on a couple of patients."

Unbelievable. "Workaholic, much?" Lia wondered.

Thomas gave her a pointed look. "Actually, now that I have other, more important things going on in my life, I plan to cut way back on my hours."

Lia's cheeks went red hot. See? She wasn't ready to face him. "Is that so?"

His level gaze never wavered. "You know that's so."

"What the heck are you two talking about?" Jalen demanded.

"Grown-up stuff." Thomas sat on the edge of the bed, reached inside the red plastic bag he'd been carrying and presented Jalen with a LEGO box. "This is for you. Why don't you put it together and give your mother a few minutes of peace and quiet?"

"Starship Enterprise!" Jalen grinned with a year's worth of delight and went to work on the box. "Cool! Thanks!"

"You're welcome."

Out in the corridor, a commotion seemed to be gaining strength.

"I don't know why I need to traipse all over this hospital trying to find my son," a male voice boomed.

"No." Thomas dropped his head and pinched the bridge of his nose, his shoulders slumping. "Please, God. Not today."

The voice continued. "First they tell me he's in one room, and then they say, no, he's left the hospital, and then someone else tells me he's up here. What kind of place is this? No, I don't need your help."

"What the—" Lia began, bemused.

Thomas raised his head and stared at her. "Run," he whispered. "While you have the chance."

Without warning, the door swung open and an elderly gentleman appeared.

"Too late," Thomas muttered bitterly, shaking his head. "Too late."

Though his hand rested on a cane, there was nothing fragile or diminished about the gent, from his rigid posture to his heavily starched white oxford shirt, down to his creased, navy trousers and the tips of the most highly polished penny loafers she'd ever seen. He surveyed the room, his steely-eyed gaze resting on all of them in turn and lingering for a long time on Lia and longer on Jalen.

"Well, well, well," he finally said, coming fully inside the room. "Don't this beat all?"

Though there was only one person this could be, Lia felt it was long past time for her to take charge and draw some boundaries. This was her son's hospital room, after all. She and Jalen's grandfather needed to come to an understanding ASAP, because she was so not the one for being bullied.

"I'm sorry." Standing, she stepped forward, frowned and crossed her arms over her chest. "Do I know you?"

The man's brows and lips flattened, morphing into the same sort of imperious glare that Thomas had given poor Dr. Brown that first day she met him. Geez. This was truly Dr. Evil to Thomas's Mini-Me. Come to think of it, all three of these males could have been the same person at different stages of life—they looked that much alike.

"Don't play dumb with me, ma'am." The Admiral stuck out his hand and they shook. "I'm Admiral Thomas Bradshaw, III, U.S. Navy, retired. And you must be the baby mama."

"Okay, Admiral." Thomas edged to her side and put a light but protective hand on her waist. His face had closed off, and she felt a thrumming rigidity running down his arm. "This isn't the deck of your ship, so you need to remember your manners."

The Admiral drew himself up, outrage bleeding out of his pores. "You want to talk to me about manners, boy? Well, it's good manners to let a man know when he has a grandson who's damn near old enough to shave."

Both Lia and Thomas stole worried glances at Jalen, who was watching the proceedings with drop-jawed interest.

"I'd planned to let you know, Admiral," Thomas said, his voice laced with ice, "just as soon as we all caught our breath. We've just found each other. And we've been a little busy, as you can see."

"Well." This explanation seemed to mollify the

Admiral somewhat, and he eased down a little, clearing his throat. "I accept your apology."

Thomas raised an eyebrow. "I wasn't aware I'd apologized."

"And I trust you'll be a better father than I was," the admiral concluded.

Thomas apparently wasn't expecting this vote of confidence, because he stilled. When he spoke again, his voice was unexpectedly hoarse. "What does that mean?"

The Admiral clasped his hands behind his back, reminding Lia of a general in the movies addressing his troops, and rocked back on his heels. He opened his mouth. He closed his mouth. Then he cleared his throat again. "It means that you need to spend time with the boy. Quality time. Take him fishing. Play touch football. Tell him you love him once or twice. So you won't… have any regrets."

The two men stared at each other, with messages passing between them that Lia couldn't fathom, although she instinctively knew that what she'd just witnessed was crucial to understanding who Thomas was and who he wanted to be. And she hoped—prayed—that Jalen's appearance in their lives might help the Bradshaw men do some healing.

"Hey, Mom," Jalen piped up in the silence, having apparently gone through all his reserves of polite and quiet behavior. "Who the heck is this guy?"

"Jalen," she said, shooting him a killing glare, "this gentleman is your grandfather. Admiral, this is Jalen. I'm Lia. And I'm going to go out on a limb and say it's a pleasure to meet you."

One corner of the Admiral's mouth twitched—was

that a smile?—and his eyes twinkled at her. "Likewise." He turned to Jalen and shook his hand. "You can call me Admiral or sir, young man. Understood?"

Jalen's eyes widened. "Okay."

"Okay, what?" snapped the Admiral.

"Okay...sir?" said Jalen.

"There you go." The Admiral studied him with something like approval in his expression. "You look like a fine young man. You study hard in school?"

"Yes, sir."

"You do your chores without complaining?"

"Yes, sir," Jalen said, darting a guilty glance at Lia. Lia gave a discreet cough. "Well, sometimes," Jalen amended.

"I expect you to do better on that," the Admiral informed him. "And you listen to your elders, don't you, son? You're not one of those obnoxious kids who yak, yak, yak all the time, just to hear their own voices, are you?"

"Ah," Jalen said, clearly thinking hard and deciding to be honest. "I'm going to work on that. Sir."

The Admiral nodded with satisfaction. "You do that. And when you've whipped yourself into shape, I'm going to take you out for the day. Down to the shipyards. You can see one of the decommissioned battleships. Would you like that, son?"

"Yeah!" Jalen breathed. "Cool!"

"Cool, what?"

"Cool, sir!"

The Admiral turned to Thomas. "This is a fine boy. We'll have no problems getting him into Annapolis."

Annapolis?

Was the Admiral already scheming to get Jalen into the naval academy?

"Ah, Admiral," Thomas began.

But the Admiral was now grinning at Jalen and pointed to the LEGO set on the bed. "*Star Trek,* eh? Kirk or Jean-Luc Picard?"

"Kirk, sir," Jalen said solemnly.

"Excellent." To Lia's astonishment, the Admiral raised his right hand and gave Jalen the Vulcan salute. "Live Long and Prosper."

Jalen beamed and repeated the gesture. "Live Long and Prosper, sir."

"How're we doing in here?" Without waiting for an answer to his cursory knock, Thomas strode later that night into Jalen's darkened hospital room, which was lit only by the flickering TV and a small floor lamp in the corner. Lia noticed he looked everywhere—at the sleeping boy, his IV, the various machines and monitors, the dirty dinner tray waiting for removal and the heavy metal patient chart sitting on the nightstand. He looked at everything but her as she sat in her chair by the bed and flipped through a magazine. "How'd he eat?"

"Very well," she said.

Still not looking at her, he reached for the chart and flipped it open, checking the boy's latest test results and vital signs.

"Good. How long's he been asleep?"

Bemused, she checked her watch. "Ten minutes or so. I think he hit a wall and just crashed."

"Hmm."

"I thought you were going home to rest," she reminded him. "Because you're, you know, recovering from having a kidney removed. Remember that? Why are you still here acting like a doctor? Didn't you say your goodbyes a little while ago?"

"I am a doctor," he said mildly. He glanced at their sleeping son, who was snuggled under his blue fleece blanket, snoring, with a growing stream of saliva trickling from one corner of his open mouth, and then flipped to another page in the chart. "I just wanted to check on him again."

"I'm so glad." The heavy sarcasm earned her a warning shot from his flashing brown eyes. "The twenty other doctors who looked in on him today all seemed like quacks."

Flipping the chart closed again, Thomas apparently decided not to dignify this comment. "His kidney function looks great. I'm really pleased about that."

What the hell was going on here? Why was Thomas acting so weird?

Oh, okay. She suddenly got it. Even though he wasn't officially on duty right now and wasn't wearing his white coat with the stethoscope slung around his neck, Thomas was wearing his doctor persona with all the accoutrements, including that brusque tone and crisp voice. Or maybe he was hiding behind it. Yeah, that was it. This was apparently what came of interactions between Thomas and the Admiral. Thomas reverted to the aloof professional who could handle anything and was fazed by nothing, probably to hide his lingering hurt feelings and childhood pain.

It was a classic defense mechanism if ever she'd seen

one. It would've worked beautifully if she weren't getting to know him so well. But she was getting to know him, and seeing him upset wasn't cool with her. Not at all.

"Why, thank you for that assessment, Dr. Bradshaw," she murmured. "I'm assuming you'll send us your bill? You take insurance, right?"

That got him. He'd been adjusting the pump attached to Jalen's IV, but now his head whipped around, and there was no mistaking the tight lines of his lips for anything other than annoyance.

"What the hell's that supposed to mean?"

"Why don't you tell me what's wrong?"

"Nothing's wrong."

"Right. That's why I can see your temple throbbing from here."

Even in the dim light, she could see his face redden with anger. Or maybe it was garden-variety embarrassment. "I don't need a shrink," he informed her. "Thanks for applying, though."

"You're so predictable. Of course the great and powerful Dr. Bradshaw doesn't need a shrink, because the great and powerful Dr. Bradshaw—"

"Knock it off."

"—doesn't have any weaknesses, does he? We established that earlier, didn't we?"

He snorted, looking to the ceiling as though he hoped divine intervention would save him from her interrogation. "Is there a point to this?"

"You have friends, don't you? People who can put up with your bravado for long periods of time and maybe talk to you every now and then? Well, why don't you treat me like a friend? Maybe we could have a conversation where you tell me what's on your mind. Wouldn't that be great? Think of the possibilities."

He hesitated, clearly torn between accepting her offer and booting her on her ass.

Sensing weakness, she continued. "I'll start. Your father is quite the character."

He stared at her, his face stony. "You have no idea."

"You're right. So why don't you tell me?"

He clammed up tight and shook his head.

"You're a tough nut to crack, aren't you? Well, let's see. I'm guessing the Admiral never missed a birthday party or a game, tucked you in bed with a story and hot chocolate every night and smothered you with hugs and kisses whenever he got the chance. Am I right?"

One corner of Thomas's mouth eased up in a fraction of a smile. "Funny."

"Really?" She popped her mouth open in an *O*, miming surprise. "Don't tell me he sucked as a father. No way!"

"He did."

"You still love him, though. Don't tell me you don't."

"What can I say? I'm stupid."

"You're not stupid. And you can see that he's trying, right?"

"I didn't spit in his eye and kick him out earlier, did I?"

"You did not. For which I think you deserve a medal."

"Damn right I do."

They stared at each other for a beat or two, smiling with their eyes if not their mouths, and Lia felt his mood lighten as dramatically as if a cloud had drifted away from the sun. The corresponding lightness in her chest—it almost felt like happiness—was crazy but undeniable.

"You're a pain in the ass, Special Agent," Thomas said.

"I try, Doctor."

"So this is what friends do, eh?" he wondered. "Pick at scabs and stare at what's underneath?"

"Friends try to help each other, yes."

Something unidentifiable changed between them; she felt the heat and flow of it even before she heard the new hitch in his voice. "You do help me. More than you know."

"Is that true?"

"Yeah."

She smiled. "Good."

Thomas glanced again at Jalen, who was still snoring, still drooling. Then he turned back to Lia. "Do friends take friends for gelato?"

"Sometimes."

"Good." By unspoken signal, they reached for each other, linking hands, and he tugged her toward the door. "Let's go."

Chapter 10

"I'm not so sure this is a good idea," Lia said.

Ah, yes. He'd known this was coming, hadn't he? He and Lia had gotten too close for her comfort in the last several days, and walking to a restaurant while holding hands was too much like a true date for her liking. Now that the immediate medical crisis had been managed, it was time for her to throw a few roadblocks his way.

Poor thing. She had no idea what she was up against or how many hoops he was willing to jump through if she was the prize. His determination knew no bounds.

"What's not a good idea?" Thomas worked hard on looking innocent and nonthreatening. "Breathing fresh air? Walking? Holding hands? Getting gelato?"

"I was talking about leaving the hospital. But now

that you mention it, holding hands isn't that bright, either."

Just in case she had any plans to pull free, he wove their fingers together, rubbing his thumb over the back of her hand. Her skin was silky, her grip strong, and he wasn't letting go yet. Period.

"And don't get me started on that whole joint nap thing. You caught me at a weak moment. You know that, right?"

"Clearly," he said sourly. "Physical contact with you is never that easy."

As he'd expected, the punishment for this snippet of honesty was the swift snatching away of her hand so she could cross both arms over her chest. Unperturbed, he reached for that hand, pulled it free and held it again.

She didn't resist. Much.

"Jalen's asleep for the night," he assured her, "and I'll have you back in an hour or so, in case he needs you."

This didn't mollify her. "You should be asleep for the night, too. Not traipsing down the street with me."

Yeah, she had a point there. His energy was definitely on the downswing, and his incision was starting to twinge a little. Well, a lot. But he didn't do the recovering-patient thing very well and wasn't one for lying around. So he changed the subject.

"I want to talk about that nap thing," he told her. "Felt good, didn't it?"

"No comment."

They'd been meandering down the sidewalk, headed for a bistro on the corner where they served drinks and gelato, and enjoying the crisp fall air, but now he stopped to face her, oblivious to any passersby. Though the light breeze was causing her hair to flutter across her face, he could see enough of her cheeks to know that they were flushed. Her brown eyes, meanwhile, had begun to smolder with an emotion that he planned to explore, if they ever got the opportunity.

"Careful, Special Agent," he murmured. "You've already admitted you like me."

"I shouldn't have. I don't know what we think we're doing here—"

Wow. Okay. Yeah.

Something snapped inside his head, probably his frustration at being right back at square one with her after the pleasure of sleeping with her supple body in his arms. He was so sick of her sidestepping and denials. Wasn't she?

Moving quickly, determined to prove his point, he did the thing he always wanted to do. He took her face between his hands and savored the feel of her. Then he leaned in and tasted those lips, which, after an initial hesitation, were yielding, tender and as eager as his.

Heat curled in his belly, and a wave of lust rocked him, so primitive he half expected to open his eyes and see a dinosaur wander by.

But now was not the time.

Shuddering with the effort, he let her go and eased back enough to see the blazing heat in her eyes and the flush in her cheeks.

"I wish you'd stop doing that."

"No, you don't," he said flatly, as irritated as he was aroused. He was gratified to see that she had the decency to lower her eyes, which was her way of conceding the point. "But speaking of wishing, I wish you'd stop sending me mixed messages. You're hot, you're cold, you look at me the way I'm looking at you, and I'm—what? Supposed to pretend I don't see it?"

"I don't want the complication of a man in my life now."

"You want me, though."

"You could have any woman you wanted. I'm sure you have had any woman you wanted. Why don't you pick one of these passing groupies who keep eyeballing you, Doctor? You'll forget about me by morning, as I'm sure you usually do with the women you sleep with."

He squeezed his eyes closed and scrunched up his face, overcome with a sudden and flaming discomfort because, much as he wished he could deny this accusation, it was true, and he'd earned it. Women noticed him; even now, he was aware of appreciative female gazes on all sides as people passed them on the sidewalk. He noticed women noticing him. Normally, he reveled in women noticing him.

But now, suddenly, it all seemed so…meaningless at best, ridiculous at worst. As though he'd spent the first half of his life as a strutting peacock and been too arrogant to even realize it.

Nice.

"Cat got your tongue?" Lia wondered.

He couldn't answer. He was too busy framing his defense.

They walked the last few feet to the hostess station at the bistro. Soon, they were seated at a little wrought-iron outdoor table under a market umbrella, looking at menus.

"So, why the silence?" Lia asked coolly, perusing the flavor choices.

He put his menu down and struggled, determined to be honest even though the right words danced just out of his reach.

"Women notice me. I like women. Win-win for everybody, right?"

"So what's the problem? Why not keep doing what makes you happy?"

Being near you makes me happy, he wanted to say, but couldn't manage it, especially with her indifferent attitude tonight. She had him seriously off-kilter, this one did. As if she wouldn't break stride if a sinkhole opened under his chair and sucked him into the center of the earth. He, meanwhile, was having increasing difficulty getting through ten minutes without her.

"I always was happy," he said, dialing back some of his annoyance.

"Until what?"

Ah, the hell with it.

"Until I saw you."

"So I make you unhappy? Is that it?"

"You make me want more."

Their unsmiling gazes connected and held, as strong and unbreakable as steel cable. Meanwhile, that dangerous chemical reaction happened between them again, sweeping all the air out of the vicinity.

"There you go again," she said softly.

Man. He couldn't even breathe, much less speak. "What?"

"Looking at me like that."

"I can't help it," he said helplessly. "I want you."

"For now."

"No." The flat denial was right there, surprising him with its vehemence.

"Pretty words are easy, Doctor."

"You'll see that I'm telling the truth soon enough."

"How's that?"

"Because I'm not going anywhere."

"Because of Jalen."

"No," he said again. "Even if there was no Jalen, I'd still be right here. With you. I'd already made up my mind to find you again before you burst into my office."

Startled, Lia flushed and looked away.

"Hello!" The bright-eyed server, probably a college student, swooped in, pouring water into their empty glasses. "How're you folks doing? Can I start you out with a drink?"

Thomas glared up at her. Did they not train these people to notice whether an important conversation was going on before they interrupted? "We're going to need a few minutes."

"Okay," she chirped. "Just so you know, the margaritas are still half off for another fifteen minutes."

"Thanks." He gave her a tight smile.

Looking mildly affronted but still way too happy, the server left, and Thomas tried to steer the conversation back into safer waters. Like maybe somewhere that wasn't so close to him spilling every single gut reaction he had to this woman before they'd even placed their order.

"What about you?"

She raised her brows. "What about me?"

A possessive streak chose that exact moment to raise

its head and wave hello. He didn't like it; it was like a lead cannonball settling into his chest. "Don't you get lonely? Don't you want someone in your life?"

"I already told you. I'm perfectly happy without all the hassle. Who needs a man?"

Yeah, okay.

He needed a second to regroup.

So that's what he was to her—a hassle? What did he have to do or say to gain some traction with Lia? Why wouldn't she give him the slightest opening? That cannonball in his chest, meantime, didn't feel like it was easing back any, and he was beginning to have the unbalanced sensation of trying to run on a greased log without landing his ass in the water.

"What the hell does that mean?" he barked.

Ah, damn. She was back to studying the menu, like the freaking gelato was more important than this conversation. Would it be rude if he snatched the thing out of her hands and threw it to the ground?

"It means that all I have time for is BOB."

"Bob?" he echoed, nearly choking on the name.

That crisp brown gaze flicked up at him before returning to the menu. "My battery-operated boyfriend. Oooh, pistachio!"

What did she just say?

Screw manners. He snatched the menu, ignoring her surprised gasp, and put it on his lap so he could have her full attention and they could bring this conversation to a satisfactory conclusion, whatever that may be. Assuming, of course, that his brain ever rebooted.

"Battery-operated boyfriend?"

She blinked at him, all bewildered innocence. "What else should I do?"

What, indeed?

While it was reassuring to know that the mother of his young and impressionable son didn't have a revolving door on her bedroom, he felt more agitated and unsettled than ever. Unbidden images of Lia crept into his mind, sprawled out on some comfy lounge chair, and settled in for a nice, long stay.

Lia alone and naked, writhing in her bed.

Lia with her eyes closed, arching, her nipples pointed toward the ceiling and her hand moving between her thighs.

Lia making herself moan.

Feeling hot and unbearably aroused, he reached for his water and gulped it down, spilling a few drops on his chin, which he swiped with a napkin. Then he drank again until the glass was empty.

She waited, unruffled.

"Are you trying to make my head explode?" he asked.

"Excuse me?"

Resting his elbows on the table, he leaned closer, lowering his voice. "Because you have to know that you've just handed me the biggest challenge of my life." Frustration made him scrub his hands over his scalp, and if he'd been thinking straight, he would've taken the opportunity to shut the hell up. But that was the thing about being with Lia: he couldn't think straight. The confessions, therefore, kept right on coming. "It's already eating my guts out to know that we have a child together, and I've never even had the pleasure of being inside you."

The ringing silence was proof that he'd said way too much, but he didn't want to take it back. Just the opposite. It felt good to tell her how he felt, as though he'd been in a cage and was now able to spread his wings and soar to freedom.

Lia, on the other hand...

Well, lookie there. Ms. Special Agent wasn't quite so cool and impervious now, was she? A vivid red flush crept over her cheeks, and she shifted in her seat. If he didn't know better, he'd think she'd just crossed her legs, possibly because she was as hot right now as he was.

"I'm not trying to be a challenge. This isn't a game. This is my life."

He stared at her, unsmiling. "Do I look like I'm playing?"

Some of her defiance wavered, and he wondered, for one terrible second, if she was going to cry. Lia was tough, though, and that vulnerability passed, leaving only that iron core of determination to keep him at arm's length for as long as she possibly could. "I am not a woman for you to screw with, Thomas. My life is fine right now, so I don't need you coming in and messing things up on a whim, even if we do want each other. So if you're just marking time or trying to play house with your baby mama or doing whatever it is you normally do with women, then find someone else, because I'm not the one for that. I have a son to raise. Oh, yes, I'll have the pistachio gelato, thanks. The large one."

She and the server, who'd rematerialized at his shoulder, both stared at him, waiting to see what he wanted and what he'd do next.

Like he knew.

He thought of his thriving practice, his house, his car and the money he had in the bank, which was a lot. He thought of his looks and his smarts, which had always gotten him whatever he wanted in life.

All that was on his side, and it still might not be enough to get him this fierce and beautiful woman.

He may not, in other words, be mature enough or man enough or have character enough to win the big prize sitting across from him. Maybe he could eventually seduce her, but her body, much as he wanted it, was only a fraction of what he was after. The rest was still formless and vague, but he wanted it. Might go so far as to say he needed it.

She wasn't impressed—not enough, anyway—and that scared the shit out of him.

The question, for the first time in his charmed, spoiled life, was this: was he worthy?

He had no freaking idea.

He felt, as he always felt when he was with Lia, as if his world had tipped just that much further off center. But then a lightning bolt of clarity hit him, and everything made sense.

"I'll have the raspberry," he told the server, determined to get rid of her. When she hurried off, he focused all his attention on Lia and gave her a wry smile.

She stiffened and frowned. "What's so funny?"

"You are."

"How's that?"

"You almost had me fooled there for a minute, but

I get it now." He paused, giving her time to squirm so that she could be as off balance as he was. That was only fair, right? "You must be awfully scared to work so hard at pushing me away."

Her face turned purple. "I'm not—"

Her bluster couldn't fool him. Not anymore. "And why are you so scared? Could it be that I'm not the only one struggling with this?"

She stilled, looking as though she didn't particularly want to ask the logical follow-up question. "With what?"

"With the feeling that you and I could have something big."

"We'll never know, because I don't want it."

Oh, she was funny. She said it like that was the end of the matter. "Wow. Most people your age have already realized we can't control everything that happens to us in life. I'm assuming you didn't want a sick kid, either, but you got one of those, didn't you?"

"Are you comparing having feelings for you to kidney failure?"

A wave of tenderness hit him, so powerful he wondered if he was already in love with this woman and thought that he probably was. She'd been on her own for so long, juggling all the balls by herself and standing strong and proud by sheer force of will. No wonder she was scared and prickly.

Not that he could read her mind or anything, but she probably figured that since life hadn't been kind to her, why would it start now? She'd had a husband; he'd died. She had a kid; he'd nearly died. Why would she trust in anything that could be good and beautiful just because Thomas had showed up on the scene?

"The thing you need to realize, Lia," he said, knowing he needed to continue to be patient and knowing it would be hard, "is that some things just happen. They just are."

Lia stared at him, her expression giving nothing away.

"Some relationships just are." He paused because the words needed time to sink in. "We just are."

Chapter 11

"Wow. This is, ah, great." Jalen eyed his ninth birthday present from Thomas, a BMX bike with fiery orange detailing and a matching helmet dangling from the handlebars, with wary eyes, as though he expected the thing to run him down and leave tire tracks all over his back. "Thanks a lot."

Lia exchanged a glance with Thomas, who looked as bewildered as she felt. This was not the ecstatic reaction they'd expected, especially after the weeks of planning and conspiring that had led up to this moment. They'd researched bikes on the web and visited all the local bike and toy stores, comparison shopped and consulted *Consumer's Digest*.

Once the model was chosen, they agonized over color choices and strategized about how best to get it into Lia's basement ahead of the birthday dinner without

Jalen noticing. They'd even found a big-ass red bow for that damn bike, and this was the excitement level it generated?

Oh, hell no.

Thomas stepped forward and gripped the handlebars for stability, so the thing wouldn't topple into the table and ruin the cake, a chocolate monstrosity with enough butter-cream-frosting balloons on it to ice another three or four cakes. "Why don't you hop on, buddy? Try it out."

Jalen kept up that game smile even as he edged back a step. "Maybe later."

"What's wrong?" Lia tried to keep it casual, but this was crazy. What kind of kid didn't scream with delirious joy when presented with a bike, especially when said kid had spent much of his life being too sick to learn to ride with all his friends? "Don't you like it?"

"Sure I like it." Jalen's guilty gaze flickered to Thomas and back, which was good. At least the boy was remembering her stern strictures about being polite when you didn't like a gift. "It's, ah, nice."

"But," Thomas prompted.

Jalen opened and shut his mouth, clearly struggling, and then seemed to decide to let loose with the honesty, which was always a dicey proposition where a kid was concerned. "But those things are crazy dangerous. No way am I getting on that."

"Are you—" Thomas, who was apparently taken aback by all this vehemence and not sure whether Jalen was serious or not, started to laugh and then thought better of it. "Are you for real?"

"Heck, yeah," said Jalen.

"But I got you a helmet. It's right there."

"Dude," Jalen said, letting out a huff of exasperation, "have you seen the statistics on emergency-room visits caused by bike accidents? I just got my kidney! I'm not trying to go back to the hospital. I mean, come on. Are you for real? The only thing more dangerous than a bike is a skateboard! Why didn't you get just me one of those and be done with it? Or maybe a rifle. Why not just get me a rifle with some ammo?"

Thomas's jaw hit the floor.

Muttering darkly, with Bones hopping along at the heels of his gym shoes, Jalen dropped back on his chair at the table, helped himself to another slice of bacon-mushroom pizza and took a giant bite.

Thomas turned to Lia, as though she had any answers.

"That's your son," she reminded him, reaching for the dessert plates. "Who wants cake?"

"I get the first piece!" Three bites into the pizza, Jalen swallowed, turned the slice around and went to work on the crust. "And I want the green balloon, okay? The green balloon."

Naturally he wanted the green balloon, which was in the dead center of the rectangular cake. How on earth was she supposed to manage that? It wouldn't do any good to point out that all the balloons would taste the same, either. Jalen was a kid and that, by definition, meant he didn't want to hear it.

"That's your son," Thomas murmured in her ear, brushing her cheek with a quick kiss as he rolled the bike into the corner by the TV, where it would be out of the way.

Lia grinned down at the cake, feeling ridiculous—*it was only a little kiss, stupid!*—and happy. They'd spent a lot of time together in the last few weeks, she and Thomas, and her breath still caught when he walked in the room, and her skin still shivered when he touched her.

She kept telling herself that that would change if—when—they finally slept together, but she didn't believe that actually having sex with him would cool things off between them. If anything, it would probably heat things up.

The heat terrified her.

Were there other terrors lurking in the corners of her mind?

Hmm. Let's see.

The way she now looked forward to talking to Thomas about everything from Jalen to the weather to politics to a new recipe she'd found, because Thomas was funny, interesting and interested, brilliant and, yes, insightful. The way she longed for him when he wasn't there. The way her body ached for him.

He was making a place for himself in her life, and that was terrifying, too.

"There you go, thinking again." Thomas was back with those keen eyes of his, skimming his fingers over the groove between her eyebrows, smoothing away a frown she hadn't realized she was making. "You should stop. You're not good at it."

She had to laugh. "Sorry. I—"

The doorbell chimed. Uh-oh. Showtime. All she could do now was pray for the best.

"Could you get that for me?" she asked him.

"Sure."

Thomas strode to the front door and opened it to reveal the Admiral standing on the porch, his shoulders squared and chin hitched high, the better to stare at everyone with his imperious gaze. Seeing who it was, Thomas stiffened.

"What the hell are you doing here?" Thomas asked after a tense beat or two.

"Thomas!" Lia hissed, but the Admiral merely raised an eyebrow at the rude welcome.

With a resigned sigh, Thomas gave the whole greeting thing another shot.

"What I meant to say, Admiral," he said in a formal voice, stepping aside and opening the door wider to let his father pass, "is, good evening. What a pleasure to see you. Do come in. Would you like some cake?"

"Too late." The Admiral, who was carrying a small square fish tank with a blue bow on top, waved a dismissive hand and strode inside with that rigid posture of his, looking as though he was leading several of his men through marching drills in front of the commander in chief. "Don't pretend you have manners, boy. We all know better."

Thomas scowled at Lia and shut the door. "I assume you invited the Admiral?"

"I did," she admitted.

"I assume you thought it was a good idea?"

"I did." She pointed. "Look. He brought Jalen a present."

"That's right. I heard about that fluffy rat you got here—" the Admiral paused to glare down at Bones, who'd hopped over to nibble on the laces of the

Admiral's polished brown oxfords "—and decided it was past time for you to get a real pet. I figure you can handle it now that you're a grown nine-year-old."

"Hi, Grandpa, sir!" Jalen, who'd finished his pizza, popped up from his chair and raced across the room to peer down into the tank, which the Admiral obligingly lowered for him. "Ooh! It's a black goldfish!"

The Admiral's brows snapped together with clear outrage at this ignorance. "This is no goldfish, young man. This is a betta fish. Spelled B-E-T-T-A. Pronounced BAY-ta. Siamese fighting fish. Meanest fish in the world. Loves to kick other bettas in the ass. That's why you can only have one per tank."

Jalen lapsed into the kind of grinning rapture you'd think he'd show for a bike. "Awesome!"

"Here you go." The Admiral handed off the tank to Jalen, who took it with the greatest care. "Feed him once a day. Clean the tank once a week. Don't kill him."

Jalen was all wide-eyed seriousness, as though reciting a solemn oath. "I won't."

The Admiral gave a sharp nod of approval. "Good man. That's a nice-looking bike you got there. You ride? You can't be a man until you know how to ride."

"Ah," Jalen began.

Thomas, perhaps sensing opportunity, spoke up and shot the boy an encouraging smile. "I'm going to teach him. Right, Jalen?"

Under the expectant gaze of his grandfather, Jalen squared his shoulders and decided to accept the challenge. "Right."

Thomas, now bursting at the seams with paternal pride, winked at the boy.

"What's his name?" Jalen asked the Admiral, turning quickly back to the most important topic at the moment: the fish.

"Pick one."

Jalen cocked his head, thinking hard. "How about Spock?"

Another nod. "Spock it is. Let's put him in your room before you drop and kill him."

Grandfather and grandson headed down the hall and disappeared up the steps, their voices still audible. "Do you like our house, sir?" Jalen asked him.

"It's not bad," came the gruff reply. "I'd like it better if it wasn't so dusty. I can see your mother isn't much of a housekeeper."

What could Lia do except laugh? "He's a gem, all right."

"You're the genius who invited him," Thomas said.

He didn't look angry or anything, but she figured a little smoothing over wouldn't hurt. "I hope you don't mind. You know Jalen calls him every day, right? They're crazy about each other."

Thomas nodded. "I can see that. The Admiral put his hand on the boy's arm. That's the rough equivalent of a bear hug from anyone else."

"Good point. So you forgive me?"

"Yeah," he said, smiling as he smoothed the hair at her temple. "Because I'm putty in your hands, in case you hadn't noticed."

Helpless to do otherwise and enthralled by the feeling of his skin on hers, she smiled back because, sometime in the last few weeks, she'd realized something important: Thomas was now in her blood, and wishing him out hadn't worked. He was also still here, just as he'd promised, and opening the door to the possibility of a relationship between them had begun to feel… safer. Not safe, exactly, but safer.

"Putty in my hands?" she repeated, tipping her smiling face up for his kiss. "That works for me."

Lia closed the book, eased the blanket away from Jalen's sleeping face so he wouldn't suffocate in the night, slid off the edge of the bed and clicked off the lamp on the nightstand.

Was she forgetting anything? A quick glance told her that Spock the fish was settling in nicely in his new spot over on the dresser. She'd have to make sure Jalen fed him first thing tomorrow. As a final act, before she was officially off mommy duty for the night, she flicked a sheet over Bones's cage. The bunny, which was snuffling against the cedar shavings, getting comfortable, wriggled his pink nose at her before he disappeared from view.

There. Done. Now she could relax until tomorrow, when it all started again.

"Well, I think the troops are finally all bedded down for the night," she said.

"Finally."

Thomas's low murmur came from the overstuffed chair in the corner. He liked to sit there while she and Jalen took turns reading aloud, his head leaned back against the cushions, eyes closed and long legs stretched halfway across the room. It was all part of the routine they'd developed in the last couple of weeks, almost like they were a family. There'd been a time or two when his breathing had evened out and she suspected he'd dozed off, but he never missed a detail and always had a ready answer if Jalen asked a question or didn't understand a word in his book.

His posture of extreme relaxation was at such odds with the brusque, professional side she saw of him at the hospital that she could hardly believe he was the same man. If she didn't know better, she'd think this was one of the favorite parts of his day.

Lia headed for the door. "I was worried he wouldn't wind down after all that pizza and cake, but he surprised me."

"I think he hit a wall."

Lia's skin prickled with delicious heat, especially up the back of her neck into her nape, something it had been doing for the last half hour or so. There was something different about Thomas tonight—a new intensity in his shadowed eyes, maybe, and a huskier edge to his voice. Even now, as he unfolded that big body from the chair and followed her into the dark hallway, there was a thrumming tension about him that resonated inside her and almost made the air vibrate.

Her hands, she saw as she turned and reached for the knob to close the door behind them, had begun to tremble with sudden jitters, and she opened her mouth, unable to stop the nervous babble.

"He and the Admiral both seemed to have a good time, don't you think?"

"Hmm," Thomas said.

He was close behind her now. Way too close. That prickling sensation sharpened, running up her scalp and down her face, making her cheeks burn and her throat tighten. He was going to press the sex issue now, because he was finally out of patience with her. And who could blame him? What kind of grown man waited this long for a woman?

God knew she couldn't wait any more. She'd fought the good fight, yeah, but she could only resist for so long when the sexiest man she'd ever known looked at her with those eyes. So now this was it. The moment of truth.

A bubble of hysteria nearly shot out of her mouth. Poor guy. She'd warned him that she hadn't had sex in nearly a decade, and therefore had fading skills that were questionable at best, but had he listened? No. Well, he was in for a major disappointment tonight, wasn't he?

Much to her horror, the chatter continued, showing no signs of slowing.

"And I thought you and the Admiral got along pretty well, except for when—"

"Shh." Without hesitation, those arms wrapped around her and settled her against a body that was marble hard and yet somehow generated the heat of a blast furnace. The globes of her butt fitted around a rigid erection and, just in case there was any doubt about what he wanted, his hands slid over the silk of her dress, one finding her breasts and the other running up her bare thigh to seek out the V between her legs.

She shuddered and sagged against him, already lost. "Oh, God," she gasped.

"There's nothing to be scared about."

Ha. Easy for him to say.

The lie popped right out. "I'm not scared."

His lips, which had found their way to her neck in a slow nuzzle, curled in an unmistakable smile she was glad she couldn't see. "Can I tell you something?"

Ah, man. His hands were causing so much separate turmoil that it was all she could do to breathe. One hand was cupping her breasts, learning their size and weight and circling her aching nipples with a relentless thumb, and the other was wreaking havoc below her waist, edging under her panties to the damp and vulnerable flesh beneath, caressing with a stroke that was rhythmic and unrelenting.

"Yes," she said.

Now his lips were at her ear, whispering words that arrowed straight to her heart. "I hate it when I have to leave here and go home at night. It's like a punishment."

Oh, God. Right there...*right there*. "It is?"

"Yes." He grazed her earlobe, pulling just enough with his sharp teeth. Down below, his hips had begun to swivel, thrusting her swollen sex deeper against those skilled fingers. "Because I belong here with you now, don't I?"

She hesitated.

"Don't I?" he insisted, nipping at the tender hollow between her neck and shoulder, making her cry out with approaching ecstasy, which was going to barrel her over any second. "Don't think about lying to me."

"Yes." Her breath was barely a pant; only his strength was keeping her upright now. "Yes."

"Yes, what?"

"Yes, you belong with me."

"Inside you."

Why argue? "Yes."

Another stroke of his fingers, which were slick and hot with her honey, started the first waves of rippling pleasure. Giving herself over to them, she let her head fall back and her eyes roll closed. Her lips began to curl into a smile, but then the ripples sharpened into piercing contractions with no beginning or end, and she exploded with a cry of astonishment.

His arms tightened around her, anchoring her to his solid weight while she rode it out. The gasping mewls kept coming, too far beyond her control to rein in. She couldn't help being loud; this was what he'd done to her, and she couldn't wait for him to do it again.

Eventually her breath came back, which was an awesome feat with him holding her in a rib-crushing grip, as though Armageddon could come and go before he ever turned her loose. She felt loose and free. Light, as though anything was possible, including, incredibly, happiness.

Turning her head to look at him over her shoulder, she tried to smile.

"Thomas," she began.

Unsmiling, he never let her finish. "I need you now. You're part of me. You know that, right?"

She stilled, too stunned to speak.

"Some things just are." He shrugged helplessly, and even in the darkness she could see the flash of turbulence in his eyes, as though he wasn't happy to find himself in this spot but didn't plan on making an escape attempt. "They just are."

Too many emotions were swirling inside her, threatening to make a break for it, so she put them all on lockdown and trusted herself with just three words: "Come with me."

Taking his hands and staring up into his hard, beautiful face, she backed her way down the hall, pulling him into her bedroom.

Chapter 12

Need grabbed Thomas in a stranglehold, leaving no room for anything other than the urge to experience everything he'd been waiting for and to do it *now*. What was it that Gordon Gekko said in the movie *Wall Street?* "Greed…is good." If that was true, then he was golden, and this was his moment to gobble up all the things he wanted.

So this was Lia's bedroom, and now he was allowed inside.

He'd glimpsed it several times from the hallway, of course, always feeling like a kid with his nose pressed up against the locked glass door of an ice cream parlor. Now, finally, he was allowed inside this intimate world and could revel in all things Lia. Shutting and locking the door behind them, he took it all in with a swift glance.

It was warm and cozy, and smelled faintly of the spicy fragrance she wore. He noticed the perfume bottles on the dresser, along with a TV in the armoire, a cookbook on the ottoman in a reading corner complete with rattan chair and a softly glowing lamp. There were pictures of Jalen in expensive frames on every flat surface, vases with flowers, a small bookshelf. And then there was the bed, king-size with one of those fancy wrought-iron headboards and topped with giant decorator pillows and matching duvet, all in earthy shades of green and gold.

Once he'd taken the edge off his curiosity about the room, he turned to his other driving needs: to touch, taste and posses. Lia was still smiling up at him with those flushed cheeks and smoldering eyes, still loose and languid following her orgasm, still pulling him toward the bed. And he couldn't touch all of her anywhere close to fast enough.

And here he'd thought he had a couple skills when it came to sex. Please. Right now, all he had were shaky hands, gasping breath and skittering pulse.

"Lia."

He sank his fingers deep into the silk of her hair, searching for the warmth of her scalp beneath, and tilted her head way back so he could have complete access to her mouth, which he took with deep, thrusting sweeps of his tongue. A remote corner of his brain was aware that his urgency was making him a little rough, and maybe he should ease up and let the poor woman catch her breath, but there was no time for that now. He'd waited too long, and there were too many possible ways for their lips to fit together, tasting and nibbling, stroking and tugging, and the taste of her—a delicious combination of white wine and buttery icing from the cake—was far too delicious for him to slow down.

More. He needed more.

Anyway, she wasn't complaining. Her sounds were a thrilling combination of gasps and mewls, all of them encouraging, and every time he pulled back enough to breathe and dive back in again, discovering her mouth from every possible angle, he saw, through his half-closed eyes, that her lips were curled in one of the most sensual smiles he'd ever seen.

"I want you." Jesus, was that him with that guttural and animalistic voice that sounded as though it belonged to a caveman? Too far gone to manage gentle, he grabbed fistfuls of her hair, learning the feel of it, and then ran his fingers over her forehead and dimpled cheeks, and across those lips that were slick and swollen now, but still smiling. "You have no idea how much I want you."

"I want you—"

That was all he let her say before he ran out of patience. This was no time for talking, not when he hadn't kissed her enough yet. He took her mouth again, yanking her up against his hungry body and rubbing his hands all over her back and then lower, kneading that round ass beneath the silky slide of her dress, and then lower again, searching for her bare thighs. They were meaty, just the way he liked them, and he stooped a little, just enough to take possession of one of her knees and hike it up around his hip. There. Just like that. He ground against her, his erection so unrelentingly hard and insistent it was a wonder his flesh didn't split down the middle.

Her panting murmurs coalesced into his name and her grasping fingers scratched up underneath the bottom of his shirt and across his back. Crazy sounds collected in his throat, rumbles of approval, and that was before she spoke.

"Thomas. I need you inside me. I need you. Need you… Need it…now. Now."

Oh, yeah. He liked hearing his buttoned-up little Lia all hot and bothered despite her cool pronouncements about not needing him or a relationship. She damn sure needed him now, didn't she? And he wasn't about to let her forget it.

"You like this?" He punctuated the end of his sentence with a sharp smack on her ass. "Huh? You need this?"

Another smile, even as her head fell back and her hips writhed against him with a growing insistence. "Yes."

He wasn't in much of a mood to be merciful. Not yet. He smacked her again with his free hand, keeping that knee wrapped around his waist with the other.

"Yeah? What about BOB? You want BOB right now?"

A disbelieving laugh. "No."

"No?" That wasn't quite vehement enough for him, and he did so like the begging. "Convince me."

He was feeling pretty powerful right about then, but that stuttered to a halt—along with his pulse—when she extricated herself from his grasping arms and, staring him straight in the face with the flash of a challenge in her eyes, dropped nimbly to her knees.

Damn.

His first instinct was to step away before he embarrassed himself with the quickest premature ejaculation ever experienced in the history of mankind. This was too much. He wanted her too much, he was already on a razor's edge and the reality of seeing her going to work on his belt and zipper with that sort of ferocious intent was a billion times better than his fantasies and way too much for him to handle right now.

"Lia," he began, choked. "I don't think—"

"Then stop thinking," she said flatly.

His brain sent some sort of a message to his body, something about stopping this before it went any further, but it got lost when she pulled down the waistband of his boxers. Cooing with appreciation, she stroked him with her soft but sure hands, and then licked him from bottom to top. That was when his brain checked out altogether.

"I want this." Her hot gaze flickered back up, nailing him right between the eyes. "I want all of this." With no further ado, she sucked him deep into her mouth's slickness as her hands slid behind him so she could dig her nails into his ass.

He felt his breath stop after a single, harsh gasp. He staggered back a half step, struggling against the relentless urge to thrust, to come. It was excruciating; it was heaven. Could too much pleasure kill a person? Induce insanity? His hands went to her bobbing head, holding it between his flexing fingers, and he panted. He groaned. He whimpered, undone in a way he'd never been before, because that was Lia on her knees before him, Lia's hot mouth sucking him and Lia's humming voice encouraging him.

His heavy head fell back, and he stared up at the ceiling through half-closed eyes, his vision blurred. The breath hissed out of his lungs and wheezed back in, and his hoarse cries kept coming, louder and louder, and there was nothing he could do to contain them, even if he'd had the strength to try.

Enough. He needed to be inside her. *Now.*

With every muscle in his body now coiled tight with strain, he pulled free of her mouth's suction. It was hard, almost impossible, given his driving urge to come. His erection strained and jutted, still reaching for her, and he moved with the focused speed of a lightning strike. He stooped and caught her under her arms, hauling her roughly to her feet and trying not to see the unmistakable triumph in the curl of her lips.

Yeah, she'd won that round, true. He'd give that to her. But the match was far from over.

Pausing only to give her another frenzied kiss, he pushed her back just enough to give him the room he needed, swept his shirt off over his head and dropped it to the floor. A beat passed; he was excruciatingly aware of her roving gaze, which was hungry as it swept over his chest and arms, and of the way her breasts heaved and her nipples pointed beneath her clothes.

Yeah, it was past time for him to be inside her.

"Take your dress off." Impatient, he bent at the waist to get rid of his pants and boxers, being careful to pull his wallet out of his back pocket and toss it onto the nightstand before he let his clothes fall. "I want to see you. *Now.*"

She flushed and hesitated, infuriating him, because why, after all this, wouldn't she know how beautiful she was to him? Did she not understand how strong his need was right now? How much he wanted her? Was this about her thinking that her waist was too wide or some such nonsense? Why did women do that to themselves?

"Don't bother being shy," he said. "It's a waste of time."

Even now, she didn't like being bossed around or the suggestion of any weakness. The command seemed to galvanize her, which was the point. Bold as a stripper now, lacking only the pole, she reached behind to unzip her dress and let it fall off her shoulders and down to the floor with a shimmy. He was still reeling from the revelation of all those juicy curves he couldn't wait to get his hands on, when she released the front clasp of her thin black bra with a flick, letting her breasts bounce free.

And there she was.

The lamp's light made her brown skin gleam with warmth. The small ovals of her breasts were tipped with prominent dark nipples the color of the world's richest coffee. She had a tiny waist, rounded belly and the kind of swelling hips that would make the perfect place for his hands to grip while she rode him. Down below—

"Take your panties off, Lia."

She complied, never breaking eye contact as she bent and wiggled her way out of a pair of black lace nothings. Then she straightened, letting him look his fill with the slightest curl at the edge of her lips, as though she was finally getting the picture of what she was doing to him and reveled in it.

Have mercy.

Down below, she was bare, letting him see that the sweet cleft between her legs was ruddy with engorgement, already slick and ready for him.

He stared, his brain emptying out. And stared and stared and stared, until there was only one thing he could say, the only thing she needed to know.

"You're perfect."

Naturally, she started to shake her head and disagree, but he was having none of it.

"Lie down," he told her. "Now."

He stepped forward, and they reached for each other, and the next thing he knew, they were tumbling onto the fluffy bed, she beneath him, and the exquisite slide of his bare skin against hers was like heaven come to life. All he could do was marvel. At the softness of her fragrant skin and the way her silky limbs twined around him without needing encouragement. At her primal pants and cries and the way she whispered his name with every gasped breath. At the thrilling way her firm breasts filled his palms and her velvety, erect nipples swelled tighter when he flicked them with his thumb.

At the unexpected but wonderful turns his life had taken since he first laid eyes on this woman.

"Lia," he said over and over again, because he couldn't stop himself. "Lia."

He wedged his way between her legs and slid down the length of her body, running his cheeks and lips all over her warm belly with one ultimate destination in mind. And then he was there, with his face rubbing against her sex and his arms locked around her waist so she could never get away.

Ignoring the insistent writhing of her hips, he paused, savoring.

Her body's fresh musk filled his nostrils, and he felt the wild rush of her scent shoot straight to his brain. Surrounding him on both sides, her thighs cradled his head, and he gave in to the urge to use his teeth and bite one. Suck it. Just as he was wondering if he was being too rough, her strangled cries of pleasure hit a new level, and that was that.

Turning to the other thigh, he sucked harder, working her with his tongue. If he left marks, too bad, so sad; she could wear a long skirt tomorrow. If she didn't like what he was doing, she wouldn't sound so ecstatic.

He had to taste her.

Dragging his hands lower, between her and the linens, he cupped that ass and angled her hips just right. Her sudden silence above him told him that her breath had caught. Good. Dipping his head, he licked his lips, flicked his tongue out and ran it over that glistening nub in a big swipe that narrowed down to swirling circles.

"Thomas."

She jackknifed, her rigid body doubling up with spasms of pleasure. He'd had it in his mind to suckle her a little, really wring her dry, but he was only human, and he'd waited all he could.

Crawling back over her, he reached for his wallet on the nightstand and the black foil package inside. Moving as quickly as he could, with hands that were too shaky to work very well—and to think he was a surgeon!—he covered himself, staring into her face the whole time.

She was panting, sweat-slicked and delicious. Her eyes were fever bright, her face flushed, her lips swollen, and the sultry way she looked at him nearly drove him out of his freaking mind.

Maybe she knew it, too, because she tried to smile, but the moment was too weighty for that. "This is good, isn't it?" she whispered. "Between us?"

Taking himself in hand, he ran the tip of his penis back and forth between the honey slickness of her folds, lubricating them both.

"*Good* doesn't begin to cover it," he said grimly.

Lately she'd become way too talented at reading his moods, and she used her mental X-ray skills on him now, brows lowering with concern as she studied him. "What?"

He hesitated. Did she understand how this one thing ate at him? How it would probably haunt him forever, as though it were an asterisk beside the single greatest achievement of his life?

"It should have been like this," he said. "When you conceived Jalen. It should have been exactly like this."

She didn't answer, but her face softened and, swear to God, it was like she was glowing, as though he'd captured the sun and held it right there in his arms.

With one hard surge, he drove himself deep into the unbearably tight center of her body and began to thrust, losing himself in her cries…in their shared pleasure… in Lia.

"Wake up." The whispered voice in Lia's ear was as persistent as the hands stroking her body were relentless. Oh, wait, and there were lips at play, too, nuzzling at the tender spot at her nape, the one that always made her squirm with pleasure. "Wake up, Lia."

Consciousness came slowly, bringing equal doses of bewilderment and contentment with it. There was a man in her bed for the first time in years. How strange.

Thomas was in her bed. How perfect.

Thomas. He was worth waking up for. She smiled into her pillow, grateful her back was to him and he couldn't see her face, and cracked her eyes open wide enough to discover that the sun's rays were trying to peep through the blinds.

They were spooned together, with her butt nestled against his groin, his muscular thighs beneath hers, the front of his body providing enough warmth to scald all down her back.

He was hard again and his hands were on the move. His bottom arm was hooked up over her shoulder, giving him access to cup and knead her breasts, and his other arm had inched its way between her thighs, spreading her open just enough to glide a couple of his long fingers back and forth over her slick and aching sex. And she was now so hopelessly hooked on his fingers, mouth and body that, despite a wild and mostly sleepless night, she couldn't wait to have him inside her. Again.

Was this how an addiction was born? If so, someone needed to get the Betty Ford Center on speed dial for her and fast.

The murmuring continued. "Lia. I need you, baby. Wake up."

Another simpering grin into her pillow. "You can't possibly need anything."

Against the back of her neck, she felt the curve of his answering smile. "Last time. And then I'll leave you alone." A pause. "For a while, anyway."

She stretched her arms high overhead, languid as a cat. "I'm tired. You didn't let me sleep."

"You can take a nap later."

"Hmm." Her surrender was a foregone conclusion, but still, he should have to work for it a little. "I'm sore."

Sore was an understatement. She was stretched and achy, her lower parts so exhausted from the relentless workout Thomas had given them that it would be a wonder if she could walk unaided when he finally let her out of bed. They'd explored each other from so many angles that they'd probably worked their way through half the positions in the *Kama Sutra*, and she was wrecked, probably forever. Never in her life had her body responded to a man like this; never before had she been this strung out on rapture.

If he wanted it, and it was in her power to give it, it was his. All he had to do was ask.

"I promise," he said, licking her ear, "that I'll be gentle."

"Well," she said, turning to straddle him so that she was on top. "If you insist."

"I insist."

But neither of them moved.

She levered high on her arms, staring down into his bright brown eyes, her hair in her face and her nipples just inches from his mouth, if he chose to partake. He stared up at her with rapt intensity, his hands gliding up and down her sides and across her back and shoulders with the gentlest, most tender touch imaginable.

And she thought, with a sweet ache of pain that centered in her chest but touched every part of her body, that she was in real danger of falling in love with this man and probably getting her heart broken, because what were the chances of a playboy surgeon settling down for good with his widowed baby mama?

Then it got worse.

"Brace yourself," he softly told her, unsmiling. "I'm about to say something corny."

"What is it?"

He didn't want to say it; she could see that. It was in the way his Adam's apple bobbed and his eyes darkened with turbulence. It was in the way he opened his mouth but couldn't produce any words for several long beats.

She waited.

"You're the best thing that's ever happened to me."

He said it so low that she read his lips more than heard it. But it was enough.

Reaching between them, she took him in her hand and eased herself down his length, impaling herself as far as she could go and shuddering with the exquisite friction.

"Show me," she said.

With a raw groan, he shifted his weight and tumbled her on her back so that he was on top, hooked one of his elbows behind one of her knees, to spread her wider and go deeper, and did just that.

Chapter 13

"Well, look who it is." An hour later, now showered and dressed and working on a batch of pancakes in the kitchen, Lia watched her sleepy son trudge down the steps and gave him the usual morning greeting. "Finally decided to wake up and join the living, did you?"

Jalen, who had Bones slung under his arm in a football hold, lowered him to the floor, waited for him to hop out of the way and yawned as he dropped onto the sofa next to Thomas. Reaching for the remote, he flipped the TV on and leaned up against his father's side, snuggling as though they'd always spent Saturday mornings together like this.

"Can you put some chocolate chips in my pancakes, Mom? And I want some bananas in them, too, okay? I think that's a good combo. But no pecans. I hate pecans."

Typical.

"Well, good morning to you, too, Sunshine." Lia flipped a pancake on the electric griddle and exchanged a nervous glance with Thomas. Showtime. They'd concocted a story to explain Thomas's presence, and it *could* fly. As long as Jalen didn't notice how loose and relaxed Thomas was this morning or the way she couldn't help smiling at inanimate objects, like the spatula and the eggs in their carton or how she and Thomas couldn't stop staring at each other and then looking away, as though the intensity of the connection was now too much for them to handle, especially when they couldn't touch each other.

Yeah. This plan was doomed.

"Ah, Jalen," Thomas began, and Lia could hear the studied nonchalance and, under that, the nervousness in his voice, "you seem to have noticed that I'm here this morning."

"Uh-huh." Jalen stared at the screen and punched another button on the remote.

"Well," Thomas continued, "in case you're interested, you mother and I were up so late last night, talking and, ah, watching movies together and stuff, that she just invited me to sleep here on the couch." He waved at the pillow and blanket crumpled to his right. After staying in bed until the last possible second, he'd jumped in the shower with her and they'd washed each other's backs. Then they'd grabbed the pillow and blanket from the linen closet and dashed down here to look innocent, getting settled minutes before Jalen appeared. "I hope you don't mind."

"I don't care." Jalen punched another button on the

remote and grinned with sudden delight. *"The Simpsons.* Awesome."

Thomas waited, staring down at Jalen. Lia nervously flipped another pancake.

They waited some more.

Nothing happened. Jalen was utterly absorbed in his show, which was one of the most beautiful things about mindless programming these days. So…was that it? No interrogation? No awkward questions?

She and Thomas exchanged a quick glance of cautious relief, and she suppressed another simpering smile with difficulty.

"Who wants a glass of orange—" she called.

"But you really should sleep in the bed with mom now that you're her boyfriend and all," Jalen said, still staring at the TV and therefore oblivious to the dropping jaws of his parents. "That's how you're supposed to do it."

Lia strode through the door and into the deserted reception area of Thomas's office, trying not to look as conspicuous as she felt, which was hard. She had it bad for the sexy doctor. Really bad. That stupid smile would not go away, even at the most inappropriate times, like when her annoying boss, Dr. Dudley, was giving her his latest round of instructions and/or suggestions for the hospital's security upgrade. The mere thought of Thomas made her cheeks flush white-hot and her breath come short. In the few short weeks since they'd become lovers, he'd turned her into Pavlov's dog. What was next? Drooling every time he smiled? At the rate things were going, it could happen.

Time had shifted on her, transforming itself into the too-short increments when she was with Thomas and the long and painful interludes when they had to go their separate ways for work and other responsibilities. Today had dragged by like an ice age, the hours slowing down to keep her from tonight's dinner alone with him. She'd barely made it to the end of the day, and now that it was six, she'd hurried over to his office building to see him again. To touch him. To breathe at last.

There he was. Standing behind the receptionist's desk with Mrs. Brennan, wearing his scrubs with the stethoscope slung around his neck, both of them staring at something on the computer screen while Mrs. Brennan, who was seated, typed. At the interruption, they both looked up. Seeing Lia, Thomas stilled, and their gazes locked. The cheery greeting she'd planned to say—*Oh, hello, I was just in the neighborhood, so I thought I'd drop in*—died a quick death.

She waited, worried she'd caught them in the middle of something important and, worse, afraid that he'd realize—if not right now, then soon—how much he meant to her.

A slow smile of quiet delight crept across his face. "Hi."

Dimpling, she tried to play it cool. Well, a little cool, anyway. "Hi."

"Hello-ooo." Mrs. Brennan divided her attention between them, twisting to look over her shoulder at Thomas and then facing Lia again with a wry smile. She raised a hand and waggled her fingers. "I do hate to interrupt a nice session of young people simpering at each other and all, but I'm here too, lovely. Perhaps you'd like to greet me?"

Snapping her gaze away from Thomas, Lia laughed. "Hello, Mrs. Brennan. How are you? Did Thomas work you too hard today?"

Mrs. Brennan heaved a long-suffering sigh. "Always, dear. Always."

"I'm sorry to hear that. I hope he's letting you go soon. Or does he chain you to your desk at night?"

Thomas snorted. "Like I could."

Mrs. Brennan shot him a severe glance. "You will pipe down, or I'll be demanding another raise."

Another snort. "You already make damn near more than I do," Thomas said. "What do you want? A pint of my blood?"

"Oh, no, not a pint." Mrs. Brennan looked back to the computer screen, typing again. "A cup will do. Now, shall we finish this report, so I can go home and you can kiss your girl? I can see you're dying to."

"You got that right," Thomas murmured, his gaze heating up and reverting back to Lia, who was, naturally, flushing again. "Why don't you wait in my office for me? I'll be right there."

"Great," Lia said.

She headed down the hall and into Thomas's office, where she plopped in one of the chairs facing his desk. Then, feeling too edgy to sit still, she got up and paced, studying his things, touching them, as though the connection with his possessions would keep him close while they were apart. University degree, med school degree and medical license, all nicely matted, framed and hanging on the far wall. His white lab coat hanging on the hook behind his door, just waiting for her to press her face into it, smelling faintly of his fresh musk. His black gym bag, tossed on the floor in the corner.

After a couple of laps of the office, she perched on the edge of his desk to wait, aware of things she hadn't bothered to notice in years, like the sweet ache of her nipples against the cups of her bra, the way her skirt rode up her legs as she sat, and the rub of her bare inner thighs against each other.

It turned out that she was, after all, still a sexual being.

Who knew?

The knob turned. The door swung open, and Thomas appeared with a deliciously disquieting light in his eyes that caused need to coil, tight and hot, in the pit of her belly.

"Hi," he said again, shutting the door behind him.

"Hi."

His focus went straight to the curve of her breasts where her ruffled blouse gave way, and then shifted lower, to her legs and painted toes in her sandals. The air grew thick, making it almost impossible for her to breathe.

He did not come closer, hovering instead near the door. "I missed you."

The old Lia, the cautious one who didn't take risks and kept her feelings and desires in perpetual lockdown behind a razor-wire fence, would have smiled coolly and said, *oh, yeah?* But the new, more courageous Lia, the one that Thomas was slowly unearthing, held his gaze and let him see the heat in her own.

"I missed you, too."

That pleased him; it was all right there in the way his eyes crinkled at the corners even if he didn't quite smile. "I've been looking forward to dinner all day."

"So have I."

"I have to cancel." His non-smile faded, leaving clear disappointment in his expression. "I was just getting ready to call you."

"Oh," she said, pleased that she could still talk when it felt like someone had taken a sledgehammer to her innards. "What's up?"

"I need to scrub in in about half an hour. Dr. Alexander's sick mother has taken a turn for the worse, so he asked me to cover for him tonight. We've got a nasty gall bladder that needs to be yanked."

"Oh. Okay. I understand."

"You do?"

"Yes."

This was a lie. She did not understand. Sure, Thomas's colleagues and patients needed him, but what about Lia's needs? Hadn't she waited patiently all day? Hadn't she stockpiled all the little things she wanted to tell him over dinner, like how well the security upgrade was going and how Jalen had been tapped for the gifted program at school? Hadn't she roped off her need to feel his hands on her body, telling herself that she only needed to make it to tonight?

How the hell was she supposed to make it through the night without him?

"I was hoping," Thomas murmured, low, "that you'd be as disappointed as I am."

"Really?" Goose bumps tiptoed over her skin, tracking up her arms and into her scalp, radiating outward in a thrilling shiver. Her voice, meanwhile, had turned husky. "Feeling needy, Doctor?"

"Yeah." He stared at her, still too far away across the room. "That's the thing about you. You make me needy."

That feeling of agitation grew. She rested her hands on the edge of the desk and shifted as she crossed her legs, making her skirt ride higher across her thighs.

Thomas tracked the movement, swallowing with a rough bob of his Adam's apple.

"That's funny," she told him. "I've been feeling a little…needy myself.

"Oh?"

"I hope I'm not coming down with something."

"Hmm."

"What should I do about that?" she wondered softly.

"Maybe I should check you out." Thomas came closer, his expression darkening with the passion she now knew so well. "I am a doctor."

"Well…if you think it's for the best."

"Oh, I do."

Reaching for the stethoscope, he hooked the tips into his ears and hovered over her, staring down at her cleavage. "I'll need you to unbutton your blouse for me."

"Really?"

"It's for your own good."

She undid one button…two buttons…three, pulling the halves of her shirt apart just enough to reveal the tops of her heaving breasts in their white lace bra. His breath turned labored and harsh as he put one hand on her back and raised the chestpiece with the other. Taking care to brush the backs of his fingers down her neck as he went, he slid the chestpiece into the valley between her breasts and listened.

"Breathe in."

She did, and the tender friction between her bra and the tips of her swollen nipples was exquisite.

"Breathe out."

Another breath, more slow torture for her, especially when he gently ran his fingers over her curves as he withdrew his hand.

Standing right there, less than a whisper away, he caged her by putting his hands on either side of her hips and looked grim.

"What is it, Doctor?"

"I'm afraid it's serious," he told her.

"Oh, no."

That glittering gaze flicked up to hers and held, melting her from the inside out. "There is one treatment. It's unorthodox, but I recommend it."

"I'll do anything," she said breathlessly. *"Anything."*

"Good decision." With one careful hand, he unhooked her knee from where it crossed the other one, edged his way between her legs and stroked his hands under her skirt and up the outsides of her thighs, to the top edges of her panties. "I'll need these."

Mesmerized by his touch, his quiet intensity, Lia rocked her hips from side to side, letting him pull her panties down, but not all the way off. Then, never breaking eye contact, he tugged her hand and pulled her along as he sank into his big leather chair and tipped it back. She straddled him, resting her knees on the padding and poising as he untied the laces of his pants and slid them and his boxers down enough to reveal an erection that was ruddy and thick.

She shuddered. "Are you sure we should do this, Doctor?"

He regarded her solemnly, lids half lowered. "It's the only way."

With that, she eased down, inch by slow inch, stifling her gasps as best she could. Somewhere in the back of her mind she wondered whether Mrs. Brennan was still out there somewhere, and if she even cared. Meanwhile Thomas hissed with approval.

When, finally, they were fitted together, both panting, eyes glazed, and he had his hands up under her skirt, anchoring her by the ass, she began to ride. Up and down, around and around, in and out, any way she could manage it, she gave herself over to the abandoned pleasure of this moment…of needing Thomas inside her…of needing Thomas.

Chapter 14

"Is this enough cheese, Mom?" Jalen asked the next night. "Huh? Does this look like enough? Mom?"

Lia, who'd just punched down the rising homemade pizza dough and was getting ready to divide it into thirds, glanced at Jalen, who stood on a stool on the other side of the kitchen. He'd insisted on grating the whole two pounds of mozzarella for make-your-own-pizza night and now had a small mountain of shredded white bits overflowing his bowl and trailing over the counter. If they started eating it tonight and cycled through their entire repertoire of Italian food—lasagna, manicotti and ravioli—it would take them about, oh, two years to use all that cheese.

"Yeah," Lia said dryly. "I think that's enough."

The sarcasm was, as usual, lost on Jalen, who was in raptures of delight over the fun-filled Friday evening he had planned for his parents. Having belatedly realized that Thomas had been eating dinner with them almost every night, he had, this morning, declared that they could have pizza, watch *Star Trek* and end the evening with batches of both brownies and popcorn.

What could be better, right?

She was excited, too; no point pretending that she wasn't. Evenings with the men in her life were the best parts of her days, no question. She watched indulgently as Jalen rearranged the bowls of toppings, fussing over the red peppers.

"I think we need another red pepper, Mom. He likes red peppers. Bones does, too, Mom. Green peppers aren't the same—"

Uh-oh. "Do not," she began sternly, looking over her shoulder, her hands still filled with dough, "give that rabbit one more piece of—"

Too late. Jalen had already stooped to feed a strip of red pepper into Bones's nibbling mouth. The rabbit, being no dummy, liked to be in the thick of things at all times, especially when something was brewing in the kitchen, and had been hovering at the bottom of the stool for several minutes now. Before she knew it, the pepper was gone as though it had never existed. G-O-N-E. Both boy and bunny were now blinking up at her with expressions of utmost innocence. For effect, Bones wriggled his little nose at her.

Rather than deliver her usual lecture about the need to control their pet's diet, Lia laughed. She couldn't help it; too much was right with her world these days to worry about little things like the BMI of their floppy-eared bunny. Jalen was fine now, aglow with the pink health that came from his powerful new kidney. He showed no signs of rejection. He didn't have to go to dialysis any more and had as bright a future as any other little boy his age.

She, meanwhile, had rediscovered a part of herself that she thought had died along with her husband all those years ago. It was okay to laugh now. Fine to feel lighthearted. Perfectly acceptable to have a man in her life and in her bed. She did not, for once, have to maintain constant vigilance against the threat of impending doom, because there was no impending doom.

Things just might, this one time, turn out okay.

"Okay, smarty," she told her son, still laughing. "Feed him all you want. See if I care. But guess who's going to be cleaning up after him if he gets with diarrhea? Not me."

Jalen stuck out his tongue and made a gagging face. "Sorry, dude," he said to Bones, whose ears twitched with anticipation. "I'm cutting you off."

Bones stared up at Jalen, waiting.

Jalen stood his ground.

Bones, apparently sensing defeat, decided to back off. He hopped under the stool and settled down, closing his eyes for a nap.

Lia finished with the dough, washed her hands and took inventory of the food. Cheese, toppings, sauce, salad in the fridge… Was she forgetting anything?

Inside her jeans pocket, her cell phone vibrated, startling her. She fished it out, saw that it was Thomas and felt her pulse kick into overdrive.

"Hi," she said. "How are you?"

"Better now that I'm hearing your voice. How was your day?"

"Not bad. What about you?"

"Eh," he said. "Hey listen. I'm going to get a drink with Stubbs and DeWinter."

Lia's smile froze with disappointment, but she did a good job of keeping her voice upbeat. "Oh, yeah?"

"Yeah. They've been giving me a fair amount of shit for neglecting them since you and I got together. I hope you don't mind."

Lia stared at all the food, the DVD in its case on the counter and her son's expression, bright with happy expectation, which was soon to be dashed like hers had just been.

"Nope," she said. "I don't mind at all."

"You sure?"

"Absolutely. Here's Jalen."

"Lia—"

Passing off the phone, Lia told herself she was being stupid. So Thomas wasn't coming tonight; big deal. She felt fairly certain that the sun would still rise in the morning. Anyway, this was what she got for assuming he'd come tonight, just because he usually came. Had he said he would come? No, he had not. Did he owe her anything more than the polite phone call he'd just given her? No, he did not. Were they free agents? Yes, they were. Had she taken him for granted? Yes, she had.

Any disappointment she was feeling was the result of her own foolishness and no more than she deserved.

And yet she still felt that niggling doubt, which was always hovering in the background. Because, let's get real, Thomas was a successful, single man with a thrilling and demanding career, a life of his own and a reputation with the ladies. Yeah, he seemed to enjoy their time together, but that was no reason for her to assume he'd always be there, was it?

After all, what were the chances that a man like him would be happy, long term, playing house with his son and baby mama?

Thomas swallowed the last of his beer, took another surreptitious glance at his watch—9:13 p.m. now, exactly two minutes after his previous time check—and wondered how soon he could leave without being rude. Not that manners mattered much with this motley crew.

"This is my round," Lucien announced, reaching into his back pocket and signaling the server with a wave.

"Are you actually dipping into your wallet?" Jerome recoiled, looking worried, and threw a protective arm in front of Thomas. "Watch out, Thomas. You don't want to get hit by any flying moths or bats. Uh-oh. There he goes. Duck!"

"No beer for you," Lucien said cheerfully, withdrawing a twenty and handing it to the server, who hovered over the table balancing her tray. "Thomas? Another Corona?"

"I'm good," Thomas said quickly. "I need to get going."

Too late.

"You know what?" Lucien, who was feeling no pain by this point, leaned back to regard the server with a solemn expression. "My buddies and I have had a long day. We worked hard. Saved a couple of lives. Let's have a man's drink, shall we? Bring out the tequila. Make it Cuervo, okay?"

Jerome rubbed his hands with gleeful anticipation.

"None for you," Lucien told him sharply, but he winked at the server as she left, and there was no question that she'd reappear in a minute with three shot glasses.

Great. Now Thomas was stuck here for another round, and who knew how long that could take with these two knuckleheads. He checked his watch again: 9:15 p.m. And a half. Just great.

What the hell was he even doing here, hanging out with the fellas when he could be at home? He realized he now thought of Lia's house as home. He could be there tucking his kid in bed, unwinding over a bottle of wine with Lia, making love with her and falling asleep while still buried deep inside her body.

He'd traded *that* for *this?*

Dragging his tired ass to a dark and musty bar with peanut shells on the floor, Kool & The Gang blaring "Ladies' Night" over the speakers and a couple of drinks while these two dished out the latest Hopewell General gossip like a couple of reporters for *Entertainment Tonight?* Really? Because they'd called him whipped and used peer pressure to guilt him into it?

Way to go, genius.

By now, Jalen was in bed, asleep, Lia was showered and sweet smelling and they were snuggled in for the night without him. Hell, even the damn bunny was there with them, probably having more fun than he was right now.

Really brilliant, Bradshaw.

The server clicked his shot glass down on the table in front of him. Feeling particularly bitter about the loss of a night with his family, he tossed it back in one hard gulp and reflected on the poor quality of his life choices today. Much as he wanted to, he couldn't blame his current unhappiness on his buddies.

The thing was, he'd thought he needed to come tonight. Why? Well, because he'd had a dark moment this afternoon, a beat or two when the fear that'd been simmering over low heat in the back of his brain suddenly rolled to a full and terrifying boil.

What was he afraid of?

All the recent changes in his life. The sudden and overwhelming responsibilities he now had. The loss of his life as a carefree single and the fact that he didn't much think of it as a loss and had been thinking thoughts that, mere weeks ago, would have been unimaginable.

Like what? Like tires, for one thing. The tires on Lia's car—

"He's going at it again," Jerome said.

"I noticed," replied Lucien. "See that glazed look in his eyes? That's always a giveaway, isn't it?"

Lia's tires were going bald and needed to be replaced. Hell, her whole car needed to be replaced. The Honda had served her well, but it was old now and it wasn't the safest thing on the road, especially when it was his woman and his boy riding in it. He wanted to buy her a new car, maybe an SUV, because Jalen would be running around with all his little friends for sports and other activities soon. But if he knew Lia, and he did, she wouldn't like him buying stuff like that for her. She was way too proud. So maybe he should trade in his BMW and get an SUV, then let her borrow it. Or maybe one of them should get a minivan.

Minivan? *Him?* Where in God's name had that idea come from?

"And he's staring off in the distance, with no focus," Jerome said. "See that?"

"I'm concerned about his fixed pupils," said Lucien.

Then there was the whole living-arrangement issue. Why were they paying two mortgages? Did that make sense when he was practically living with them? No, it did not. He was thinking of selling his house and moving into hers, not that he'd said any of this to Lia yet. Or maybe selling both houses and buying a new one, because his house was a bachelor pad and the thought of his boy climbing and dangling from all the metal railings gave him the chills.

Living with a woman? With a kid? Him?

Yeah, right.

Terrifying.

Actually, his thoughts about their joint and combined future didn't terrify him. No. It was his absolute certainty that he and Lia belonged together. *That* terrified him. What basis did he have for thinking he could be a successful partner and father? Because of the stellar example the Admiral had set for him?

Yeah. Sure.

Bottom line? He knew how to be a good surgeon, and that was about it.

And what about—

Sudden raucous laughter cut across his thoughts and brought him back to the here and now at the table, where

Lucien and Jerome were staring at him, damn near doubled up with convulsions.

"What's so funny?" Thomas asked, like he really wanted to know.

"You're an embarrassment, Bradshaw. You know that? Why don't you go on home, you whipped punk? Hold a ball of yarn for Lia while she knits or take the garbage out. Get outta our sight."

"You make us sick," Lucien added. The fact that Lucien was madly in love with his fiancée didn't keep him from talking shit to Thomas. Hell, he was probably relieved there was another whipped man around to take the heat off him. "We don't want to be seen with you."

"Please." Thomas had to laugh as he got up and, just for fun, snatched up Lucien's shot of tequila and drained it down before he could register a protest. "I've got more testosterone in my little fingernail than you two clowns put together."

This caused the conversation to degenerate further into good-natured jeers and insults, and Thomas was still laughing when his cell phone vibrated in the pocket of his slacks. Checking the display, he smiled wider when he realized it was Lia.

Jerome rolled his eyes with mock disgust. "Bradshaw's out past his curfew, man," he told Lucien. "He's in for a smackdown when he gets home."

Thomas turned his back on them and spoke into the phone. "Hey. I was just about to call you."

"Hi." There was a shaky quality to Lia's voice, which made unease slither up his back. "Thank God I caught you."

"What is it?"

"It's Jalen." Her shuddering breath told him she was barely keeping it together. She paused, and then she spoke the darkest fears of any parent of a transplant patient. "I had to bring him to the E.R. He's running a fever. I'm afraid he's rejecting his kidney."

Lia trudged down the steps and into the softly lit living room later that night, feeling as though she'd just crossed the finish line of a triathlon only to be hit by a speeding freight train and dragged several miles. Thomas, who was in the kitchen hovering over a tea-kettle, didn't look much better. His eyes were shadowed, and his face was tight with strain. Yeah, they were both running on fumes. There was nothing like a health scare with your kid for taking fifteen good years off your life.

Collapsing onto the sofa, she watched as he fixed her a cup of her favorite chamomile and then topped it off with what looked like two inches of Scotch from a bottle she'd forgotten she had. For himself, he poured only Scotch into a mug, drained it in a gulp or two, gasped, then filled and drank again. He walked in silence to the sofa, sat beside her and passed her the steaming tea.

At three in the morning, drinking anything with alcohol in it was a bad idea, especially since they were just back from the E.R. One sip would keep her awake for hours and anything more than that would put her instantly to sleep for about fifteen minutes, and then she'd be awake for what was left of the night. Plus, with a sick kid in the house, she needed to keep her wits about her, and God knew she was already edgy enough, filled with a gnawing agitation that made her wonder when her nerves would start snapping like the strings on Charlie Daniels's fiddle.

On the other hand, she'd just been catapulted back into the nightmare of wondering if her kid was going to become deathly sick and die before she could do anything to help him, and she needed something to help her cope.

She drank deeply, scalding her mouth in the process.

"Hey." Thomas, his brow furrowed with worry, put one big hand on the back of her neck, working her nape with those strong fingers in a futile attempt to soothe her. "Take it easy. Everything's fine."

Sure. That was the kind of bullshit commentary that drove her through the roof. She shifted down the sofa and out of his reach, throwing up one hand in a defensive move. She saw his jaw tighten.

"Everything is not fine."

"It's just sinusitis, Lia. His kidney function is great."

"Thanks for the reminder." She drank again, nearly choking against the burn as the Scotch tracked its way down her esophagus. "You'd think I'd know the difference between a rejected kidney and a sinus infection, but no. Good thing the poor kid's father is a trained medical professional, eh?"

"Why are you being so hard on yourself? Either one can cause a fever. And you thought his congestion was caused by his seasonal allergies. You took the cautious approach, which was absolutely the right thing to do with a transplant kid. No damage done."

"You don't get it." What was with his calm and patient routine? Did he not understand that his logic, in combination with her blind mother's panic, was about to make her head explode? "Everything was fine *this time*. Jalen got sent home *this time*. Jalen didn't reject the kidney that you sacrificed for him *this time*. But *next* time…?"

"Hell, next time he may get flattened by a falling satellite on his way to the hospital. We'll take each day as it comes. That's the best we can do, Lia."

"You still don't get it," she cried.

Putting his cup on the coffee table in a gesture that was as tired as a hundred-year-old man at bedtime, Thomas sighed, rested his elbows on his knees and put his face in his hands. After a long minute, he sat up, scrubbed his hands over his head and stared at her with those weary eyes.

"Help me get it, Lia," he said quietly.

"You want to get it? Here's the bottom line. I'm an idiot."

"What?"

"That's right. I'm an idiot. You know why? Because I thought that Jalen would get his kidney and he'd be fine, and we'd be finished with sickness and fear for the rest of our lives." A burst of wild laughter surged up her throat. "Stupid, eh?"

"Lia—"

"But, hey! Now I've had the dose of reality I needed, haven't I? It's like God has tapped me on the shoulder with a reminder. *Hey, you big dummy! Don't forget that things never work out well for you and your family in the end. Maybe not today, but one day, Jalen probably will reject that kidney, and then you'll be back to square one. You may have peaceful moments or happy moments, but, hey, don't get comfortable because they won't last. Don't get your hopes up, girl, okay?"*

The ringing silence following her hysterical outburst only made her feel crazier. The wheels spun in Thomas's mind—she could almost hear them—as he worked on a response that wouldn't set her off again. Poor man. She wanted to tell him not to bother.

"Lia." He put a hand on her knee, and that gentle caress, when she was feeling so unhinged, was like the touch of a hot poker. She jerked away, and Thomas's clear frustration made him snatch that hand back and clench it into a white-knuckled fist. Still, he tried. "I don't have any magical words of comfort for you. I wish I did, but I don't. Jalen's picture is much brighter now, but he'll always have health issues that we'll have to monitor. But we're in this together now, and I—"

"Together?" This time her laughter was bitter. Derisive. "We weren't together earlier, when I was wondering whether it was my imagination that Jalen's forehead felt hot, and then later, when I was wondering whether I should take him to the hospital or not. You were out drinking with your friends, and I was where I always am—alone and scared with a sick kid!"

Thomas stilled and stared at her, his face slowly hardening to stone.

She stared back, knowing her exhaustion was clouding her judgment, making her defiant and reckless, and the alcohol was only feeding the ugliness spewing out of her mouth, but she couldn't rein herself in.

He spoke first, his voice deathly quiet.

"Is that why you haven't let me touch you all night?"

She turned her head and said nothing.

"Is there some other issue we need to address, Lia?"

"No."

His jaw tightened. "You sure?"

"Nope," she said, shrugging with all the nonchalance she could fake. "Like I said—tonight, I got a wake-up call. Jalen will always have health issues, and I'll always have just myself to rely on. End of story."

"Who says?"

Great. Now she'd gone and made him feel guilty and defensive. Possibly he also felt sorry for her, and she couldn't have that. "Look. I understand. It's no big deal—"

"No big deal?"

"No. You've got your high-powered career and your friends, and you probably have all kinds of women on standby."

"Excuse me?"

"They're probably just waiting for your call, and the last thing I want is for you to feel tied to me because of Jalen. We don't need a *Jerry McGuire* situation here."

His mouth dropped open, but his words were on a five-second delay. "*Jerry McGuire?* What the hell does that have to do with us?"

Did she have to spell it out? Draw him a graph or a picture? What?

"I always thought that Jerry fell in love with the kid. He only took the mom because she was a package deal with the kid. Let's not go down this road here, okay?"

Thomas recoiled, flinching as though he'd felt the splash of invisible but icy water on his face. Blinking, he looked away, and his profile was a collection of harsh lines and planes, except for his lips, which were twisted.

After a minute, he got up and took his time facing her. She stood, too.

"I'm leaving," he told her.

Yeah. She'd expected as much, but it still felt like a blow. "Good idea."

Despite the turbulence in his gaze, his voice was calm and even. "I can see that you're overwrought and not thinking clearly."

"Don't you patronize me," she warned in a low voice.

"Nothing I can say right now will get through to you. So it's best if I leave before things get any worse."

He headed for the door, which was what she thought she wanted. But the sight of him going made her chest tighten with fear, and it was all she could do to keep her lips pressed together and hold back the sobs that wanted to erupt.

With his hand on the knob, he turned back, and she found that she couldn't make eye contact with him. It hurt too much. So she studied the far wall instead.

"But I'll be back, Lia. Oh, and by the way? When I was drinking with my friends tonight, I wasn't trying to escape or find another hookup or recapture my glorious bachelor days. I was wishing I was here with you and Jalen. You know—my family. Just in case you're interested. So I'm not going to let your fear ruin things between us. Do you understand that?"

His...*family?* Did he mean that?

Still reeling from the use of that precious word, Lia watched as he slipped out the door and into the night's absolute blackness.

"I'll be back," he promised again as he disappeared down the porch steps.

Chapter 15

Rarely had a bike-riding lesson turned into such an unmitigated disaster.

"Jalen," Thomas said, hanging on to his patience and his quiet voice by a fraying thread, "there's no need to stop dead every time you realize you're actually pedaling. I'm holding the seat. I won't let you fall. Just keep going."

"I can't do it." Jalen, who was straddling the bike on the sidewalk, crossed his arms over his chest and worked on his sulky expression. There went the pursed lips and stony jaw. He had the sullen-kid thing just about perfected, and all at the tender age of nine. "I told you I needed training wheels."

They were out in front of Thomas's house, where they'd been for a whopping ten minutes with little appreciable progress. The tri-generational bike-riding lesson had seemed like a good idea on paper, a fun way for him to spend a Saturday afternoon with both his father and his son, but Thomas had forgotten to take their personalities and his own black mood into account. The result? The bickering was outrunning the bike riding by a ratio of a hundred to one.

"You don't need training wheels, boy." The Admiral poked Jalen in the chest with his forefinger, a gesture that Thomas remembered well from his own childhood. His breastbone probably still had the divots to prove it. "You just need to stop whining and practice. Now get back up on that bike."

"I need a break, sir," Jalen insisted.

"Oh, no," the Admiral said, shaking his head. "We barely just started up out here, and you haven't earned a break. No grandson of mine is going to quit in the middle of a lesson."

"Okay," Thomas interceded. "Let's try to focus—"

"I hate this stupid bike," Jalen cried.

The Admiral's jaw dropped. "Don't you curse this bike! It's not the bike's fault that you're a quitter."

"I am not a quitter! I need to go in the house and get a drink."

"Okay!" Thomas roared, abandoning all hopes of remaining civil. It was hot out here, he was tired, and these two clowns were driving him crazy with the sniping. "That's it! This lesson is over! If you don't want to learn to ride the bike, Jalen, then that's fine. I'll donate the thing to charity and be done with it. How's that for a solution?"

Jalen and the Admiral exchanged raised-eyebrow looks, as though Thomas was the one with issues.

"What's his problem?" the Admiral asked Jalen.

Jalen shrugged, reaching under his helmet to scratch his forehead. "I dunno. He and mom are in some big fight. They're not talking to each other."

The Admiral's speculative gaze swung around to Thomas. "Really?"

To Thomas's further irritation, he found himself flushing with embarrassment. "No," he said, swiping at his sweaty forehead with the back of his arm. "We have a couple of issues, but we're working them out. Not that that has anything to do with you two."

Issues. Thomas gave a mental snort. Was it an issue when the woman in your life suddenly wanted nothing to do with you? What about when you thought of her every minute of every day, missing her with a hollow ache that made you wonder if your soul had been lost, and yet couldn't get past your own fear long enough to reach out to her? Was that an issue? Or was it a big freaking disaster of epic proportions?

His money was on disaster.

Not that he knew what to do about it. Hell, he still wasn't quite sure how they'd ended up at this point. All he knew was that he'd stopped being able to breathe three nights ago, after he'd left Lia's, and hadn't figured out a way to get back what he needed.

Which was not good for his mood.

The Admiral, much to Thomas's surprise, turned to Jalen and pointed him toward the house. "Why don't you hop down now? Take a little break. In fact, why don't you scuttle on inside and bring us out some lemonade or something? Make yourself useful."

"Yay!"

With no additional encouragement, Jalen dropped the bike to the grass, sprinted to the front door and disappeared inside with such glee that Thomas wondered if they'd ever see him again. And then he wondered why the Admiral was looking at him like that.

"What?" Thomas demanded.

The Admiral's eyes were narrowed and shrewd as he studied him but also, beneath that, kind. Maybe even a little sympathetic. "Lia's a good woman, Thomas. She reminds me of your mama that way."

Sudden emotion caught Thomas so tight around the throat that he didn't dare risk answering. It hadn't occurred to him to put Lia and Mama together, but now that the Admiral mentioned it... Yeah. They had that same steely core of strength, that same warmth. The Admiral was still waiting for a response, he realized, but he didn't have one. The best he could do was nod.

"I was hoping she'd be around for a long time."

Thomas cleared his throat. "You and me both."

Both a little gruff now, the men stood side by side, shoved their hands in their pockets and watched a couple of cars as they passed.

After a while, the Admiral spoke again. "Well, one thing fixes up a world of hurt, son. You'd better remind her that you love her."

Love?

Wait—*what?*

Love... Love... Love. The word echoed through Thomas's brain like a cannon's boom inside a cave. But...love?

Sudden clarity zinged him like a touch from a TASER.

Yeah, you dumb shit. Love. Of course.

Was that what he'd been afraid of these last few days? Putting a word to the feelings? Understanding the full implications of the way he felt? Telling her? Succumbing to it and riding the wave all the way to happiness? What the hell was his problem?

"Ah," he stammered.

The Admiral gaped at him. "You have told her, haven't you?"

"Well…"

"God almighty." In a gesture of purest disgust, the Admiral smacked a palm to his own forehead. "I've raised a half-wit."

Yeah, Thomas thought, running his hand over his head and wishing lightning would strike him down on the spot. That about covered it.

Just then, Jalen banged back through the screen door and bounded through the grass with three bottles of lemonade clutched to his chest. "Here you go, Admiral, sir. This one's mine. Here's yours, Thomas."

The Admiral had already opened his and was taking a giant swig, but now he choked and stared down at Jalen. "Did I just hear you call your father *Thomas?*"

"Uh, yeah," Jalen replied, looking wary.

"That's your daddy, boy! You call him *Dad.* You hear me?"

Jalen, looking up at his grandfather with honest bewilderment, hit him with the kind of childish question that strips you bare and exposes you to raw truth, whether you're ready for it or not.

"Why should I? Thomas doesn't call *you* Dad."

The Admiral blinked, his face undergoing a slow transformation to purple.

Thomas shuffled his feet, undone by this kid who was so much wiser than he was.

Jalen waited for his answer.

At last, the Admiral swiped at his nose with the back of his hand and cleared his throat. "You're right about that, young man. Maybe if I work on being a better father, he'll start to call me *Dad*. What do you think?"

Jalen shrugged, looking unsure, but hopeful. "You never know until you try."

"That's right." The Admiral glanced across the top of Jalen's head and winked at Thomas. "You never know until you try."

"I think I could work on calling you...*Dad*," Thomas said, not knowing where the words were coming from, even as he said them. But there was something deeply comforting about receiving advice in a timely manner from his father, something almost normal about it, and he wanted more of that. Hell, he'd been waiting his whole life for it. Anyway, wasn't this a time for new beginnings in his life? "If you don't mind, that is," he added quickly, seeing the Admiral's arrested expression.

The Admiral's expression softened, and he looked almost touched. "I don't mind," he said gruffly, clapping a hand on Thomas's shoulder.

Thomas swallowed hard, trying to master all these unruly emotions.

"You know, Thomas," Jalen said, looking thoughtful with his chin cupped between his thumb and forefinger, "I've known you for a while now. You're not a bad guy. Maybe I should start calling you...*Papi.*"

"*Papi?*"

"Well, that's what my friend Emilio calls his dad," Jalen explained, doing that shrinking-into-his-skin thing kids do when they think they've said the wrong thing. "It's Spanish for *daddy.* I think it might be a nickname for *padre* or something. But if you don't like it—"

"I like it," Thomas said quickly, struggling against that lump in his throat again. "I like it a lot."

"Okay, *Papi!*"

The Admiral, perhaps seeing that Thomas was about to lose it, decided to intercede. "Now let's get you back up on this bike, young man, okay?"

Jalen heaved a martyred sigh and hefted the bike up off the grass. "Okay."

"I'll hold your seat this time. Your father needs to stand here and think about how he's going to fix things with your mama."

"That's easy." Jalen swung his leg over the seat and started to pedal. "He just needs to marry her. That always fixes things on TV. Then we'll be, like, an official family with a license and everything."

Grandfather and grandson took off down the sidewalk, leaving yet another word to reverberate inside Thomas's overloaded brain, throwing his world off-kilter.

Marry... Marry... Marry.

Dr. Dudley intercepted Lia outside her office just as she was returning from the cafeteria with her lunch, forcing her to stifle a groan. It'd be just like him to manufacture an alleged hiccup in the new security system she'd designed and then force her to stick around for another month or so, troubleshooting nothing because the system was glitch free, but he surprised her.

"Last day at the hospital, eh, Lia?"

"Last day."

"I owe you an apology, I think."

"How's that?"

The old man tapped a forefinger against his lips, looking thoughtful. "Well, you came to the hospital and worked hard. You built us a system that should keep everyone out, even you."

She couldn't stop a grin.

"You were a pleasure to work with, and I now understand why you did it in the first place. Because of your son. So, I apologize for being so hard on you your first day."

"Thank you." She said softly, feeling awkward and unaccountably touched. Everything got her choked up these days. She blamed Thomas—well, Thomas and herself—and the unfortunate scene the other night, when she drove him away.

Despite his vow, he hadn't come back, and she couldn't say she blamed him. Who wanted to come back to a woman who couldn't handle a minor medical crisis or her liquor without lapsing into overwrought hysteria?

But Dr. Dudley was the issue right now, not Thomas.

God knew she wasn't a fan of her temporary boss and hadn't appreciated being under his thumb, but, on the other hand, she hadn't expected him to be big enough to apologize for his harsh treatment of her that first day.

"And you have to know. I'd never have done something like that if my son's life didn't depend on it."

"I understand," he said silkily, moving closer.

Uh-oh. Here it came, she thought, bracing herself.

"Why don't we have a drink tonight? Celebrate the successful completion of your job here at the hospital? My treat. Maybe get a bite after."

Wow. And to think this Rico Suave routine worked on Nurse Tsang. Lia gave him the cold eye, which she hated to do when she'd almost made a clean getaway.

"Dr. Dudley," she said sweetly, "don't make me threaten you with my Glock again."

"Fair enough, Lia." He laughed and waved as he headed off down the hall, proving he was a good sport even if he was a horny old goat. "Fair enough."

"That was close," Lia muttered, ducking into her office and closing the door. She just had time to gulp down her salad and then—

Hang on. What was that on her desk?

Dumb question. She knew what it was, and her pulse was already galloping accordingly. Wrapped with a white satin ribbon and sitting in the middle of her neat desk on top of the blotter was a small, flat box of the eggshell blue that belonged, as every woman knew, to only one store in the world: Tiffany & Co.

Was it from Thomas? Or was this Dr. Dudley's parting gambit for sex? She wouldn't put it past the old bastard. Creeping closer, she put her salad down and reached for the box, afraid to get her hopes up. The ribbon took a while to undo, what with her shaking hands and all, and then she had it off and the box open, and her heart did a crazy flip of joy.

It was a necklace. At the end of a delicate chain dangled a glittering key pendant, and the top of the key was shaped like a heart. She'd spent enough time mooning over the Tiffany catalogs she periodically got in the mail to know that she was holding platinum and diamonds—a lot of them—in her hands, but that wasn't what made the gift so precious to her. It was the accompanying card scrawled with Thomas's handwriting that made her, quite simply, the happiest she'd ever been in her life:

Beautiful Lia:
Please take good care of this for me. It's the key to my heart.
With love,
T
P.S. Dinner 7 p.m. tonight at my house. Don't be late. The Admiral will watch Jalen.

Chapter 16

At six fifty-nine that night, Lia reached for the knocker on Thomas's front door.

The door swung open, and there—oh, God—he was.

They both stilled. Lia couldn't seem to get a handle on her breath, and the harsh rise and fall of his chest told her he wasn't doing much better. There were things she'd come to tell him, but they were too big to fit into neat little sentences, even if she could get her voice to work. And he was burning her with that intense gaze again, urgently searching her face for something he shouldn't have to wonder about or fight for. Not anymore.

"I love you," she told him, touching the warm key where it lay in the hollow of her collarbone. "I love you."

His expression brightened, and his mouth twisted, caught between a choked cry and a relieved grin.

Emotion won. The last thing she saw before he yanked her over the threshold and into his arms was the glittering sparkle of his tears.

"I love you, too." His voice was husky. Raw. "I love you, too."

"I'm sorry." She clung to his neck, kissing his forehead and cheeks as he hugged her around the waist until only the tips of her toes brushed the floor. He swung her around, to the nearest chair in the foyer. He sat, settling her in his lap, across the unyielding length of his thighs. "I didn't mean to pick a fight with you the other night. I'm not sure what got into me. I was just so scared and—"

"Shh," he said, and though tears streaked his cheeks now, his smile was wide, grooved on either side by those boyish dimples she loved so much. "You don't have to explain anything. I understand."

"But—"

Too late. Planting his hands on her cheeks, he pulled her face down for the kind of wild, nearly frantic kiss that made words unnecessary. She ran her hands all over his back, arms and shoulders, rediscovering the flex and play of his muscles beneath her fingers. He did the same, gripping her hips with hard fingers that couldn't seem to anchor her close enough. It had been way too long since they'd touched each other, and her blood went from slow simmer to raging boil in half a second. With desire fogging her vision, she went to work undoing the top button of his starched shirt, and that was when she heard it.

"A-hem."

"Oh, God." Breaking away from Thomas, Lia looked

around and discovered a woman standing there, watching them with flushed cheeks and a bemused grin. "Who the hell is that?"

Thomas wasn't quite finished nuzzling yet. Rubbing his lips across her cheek for a last lingering kiss, he sighed and turned toward the woman, still keeping Lia on his lap.

"Caterer," he said.

"Caterer?" Lia echoed blankly, registering the woman's regulation white shirt and black slacks. "Why on earth is there a caterer— Oh."

The house had been transformed, she discovered. Dozens of tall white candles now flickered along the balcony railings, down the edge of the staircase, on the mantel and on the table. Oh, man. And look at all that amazing food! Cheeses and grapes in red and green, salads and pastas, grilled chicken and what looked like sea bass next to a platter of rare tenderloin. There were decorated cookies and fruit tarts, a chocolate fountain with strawberries and pretzels for dipping and a coconut cake with icing that had to be an inch thick. Two bottles of red wine were open and breathing, and there were bowls of salted nuts and powdered truffles, in case either of them had an inch of stomach space left after all the other food had been consumed.

Standing and turning in a slow circle, Lia struggled to take it all in. "Oh. My. God."

Thomas and the caterer exchanged jubilant grins.

There was more.

Gorgeous blue and purple pom-poms of hydrangeas occupied huge glass bowls on every available flat surface: the coffee table, the end tables, in the corners of the rooms. She'd never seen so many flowers. She'd had no idea there could be so many flowers.

It was breathtaking.

Putting a hand to her chest, she pressed her heart to keep it from bursting out of her chest. "Thomas," she began, turning back to him. "I can't believe—"

He wasn't there. Well, actually, he was there. On his knees now.

"Oh, my God," she said again, because a man on his knees with another Tiffany box, a tiny one this time, could mean only one thing.

The caterer slipped away, back into the kitchen.

"So," Thomas said, taking her hands in his free one and staring up at her. "Did I mention I'm a classic over-achiever?"

Laughing and crying, she swiped at her sudden tears. "You did say something about that one time, yeah."

"I wanted tonight to be special."

"I'd say you succeeded. Big time."

"Yeah?"

"Oh, yeah. And, I don't mean to rush you, but was there something you wanted to ask me?"

"Yeah," he said, and now it was his turn to swipe at his eyes, even though he was smiling. "So, you know I'm kind of an idiot sometimes—"

"Idiot?"

"You shouldn't have to wonder how I feel about you. I should have told you I loved you a long time ago."

"Yeah? When?"

He cocked his head, considering. "Probably when you stormed into my office that first day. Possibly the first time we kissed. Definitely when you were there when I woke up after the surgery. I shouldn't've taken until now to say it."

"Oh, well," she said, shrugging. "Book smart but no common sense. What can you do?"

"You could marry me, couldn't you? Do me the greatest honor of my life?"

"I think that can be managed, yes."

"Yes?"

"Yes."

"Good." Opening the box, he produced a huge diamond ring.

"Oh, my God," she cried. "Is that—"

"Heart-shaped, yeah." No longer smiling, he took the ring and slid it onto her finger. It was a perfect fit. "It represents my heart, so you should keep it with you. Because that's where my heart always is. You know that, don't you?"

Did she know it? Staring into his shining eyes, there couldn't be any question. "Yeah."

Thomas stood, opening his arms to her, and they swayed together for a minute, clinging to each other and their new life together. And then, suddenly, they were kissing and laughing, and it seemed like a good idea to confirm recent events, because she'd hate to wake up in a minute and discover that this had all been a dream.

"So, we're getting married?"

"We're getting married," Thomas said. "And I've got a lead on a best man—if we can find him a small enough tuxedo."

* * * * *

HOPEWELL GENERAL
A PRESCRIPTION FOR PASSION

Book #1
by *New York Times* and *USA TODAY*
bestselling author
BRENDA JACKSON
IN THE DOCTOR'S BED
August 2011

Book #2
by
ANN CHRISTOPHER
THE SURGEON'S SECRET BABY
September 2011

Book #3
by
MAUREEN SMITH
ROMANCING THE M.D.
October 2011

Book #4
by *Essence* bestselling author
JACQUELIN THOMAS
CASE OF DESIRE
November 2011

KIMANI
ROMANCE

www.kimanipress.com

KPHGSP

USA TODAY
Bestselling Author

Kayla Perrin

Taste
OF
DESIRE

Salina Brown's dream job of becoming a chef is more difficult than she ever imagined. But when a nanny position comes her way, it's the perfect opportunity to dish up culinary delights in the family's kitchen. Widowed father Jake McKnight can't help but relax his guard around his new nanny. She's able to melt his tough exterior but he's still grief stricken. Can he persuade Salina to believe in their special love?

"Perrin's strong characters and even stronger storyline make this a keeper of a novel."
—*RT Book Reviews* on *Island Fantasy*

Coming the first week of September 2011 wherever books are sold.

KIMANI™
ROMANCE

www.kimanipress.com

KPKP2240911

Together they're making beautiful music…

Private Melody

Fan Favorite Author
AlTonya Washington

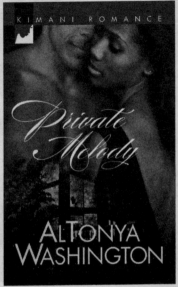

Kianti Lawrence has struggled hard to become a major force in the performing world. Music is her life…until the beloved, world-renowned pianist meets a man who shows her what she's been missing. Something about handsome, powerful former ambassador Therin Rucker strikes a harmonious—and seductive—chord. Can he make her see that the passion they're making is the truest music there is?

"Hot and steamy sex scenes and undeniable passion will leave readers panting and eager to read this book from cover to cover in one night."

—*RT Book Reviews* on *Every Chance I Get*

Coming the first week of September 2011 wherever books are sold.

KIMANI
ROMANCE

www.kimanipress.com

KPAW2260911

KIMANI ROMANCE

FARRAH ROCHON

Field of **PLEASURE**

Field of **PLEASURE**

FARRAH ROCHON

Life is one endless touchdown for Jared Dawson—until the former playboy and star cornerback discovers his girlfriend's infidelity. Reeling from the betrayal, Jared returns to his player ways. But when he meets Chyna McCrea, the game is off, as he falls fast and hard. Can Jared and Chyna score the greatest victory of all, by being on the winning team of love?

"This is a real page-turner."
—*RT Book Reviews* on *Huddle with Me Tonight*

KIMANI HOTTIES
✳ MARRYING THE MILLIONAIRE ✳

It's All About Our Men

*Coming the first week of September 2011
wherever books are sold.*

www.kimanipress.com

KIMANI™ ROMANCE

KPFR2270911

REQUEST YOUR FREE BOOKS!

2 FREE NOVELS
PLUS 2 FREE GIFTS!

KIMANI™ ROMANCE

Love's ultimate destination!

YES! Please send me 2 FREE Kimani™ Romance novels and my 2 FREE gifts (gifts are worth about $10). After receiving them, if I don't wish to receive any more books, I can return the shipping statement marked "cancel." If I don't cancel, I will receive 4 brand-new novels every month and be billed just $4.94 per book in the U.S. or $5.49 per book in Canada. That's a saving of at least 21% off the cover price. It's quite a bargain! Shipping and handling is just 50¢ per book in the U.S. and 75¢ per book in Canada.* I understand that accepting the 2 free books and gifts places me under no obligation to buy anything. I can always return a shipment and cancel at any time. Even if I never buy another book, the two free books and gifts are mine to keep forever.

168/368 XDN FEJR

Name	(PLEASE PRINT)	

Address		Apt. #

City	State/Prov.	Zip/Postal Code

Signature (if under 18, a parent or guardian must sign)

Mail to the **Reader Service**:
IN U.S.A.: P.O. Box 1867, Buffalo, NY 14240-1867
IN CANADA: P.O. Box 609, Fort Erie, Ontario L2A 5X3

Not valid for current subscribers to Kimani Romance books.

Want to try two free books from another line?
Call 1-800-873-8635 or visit www.ReaderService.com.

* Terms and prices subject to change without notice. Prices do not include applicable taxes. Sales tax applicable in N.Y. Canadian residents will be charged applicable taxes. Offer not valid in Quebec. This offer is limited to one order per household. All orders subject to credit approval. Credit or debit balances in a customer's account(s) may be offset by any other outstanding balance owed by or to the customer. Please allow 4 to 6 weeks for delivery. Offer available while quantities last.

Your Privacy—The Reader Service is committed to protecting your privacy. Our Privacy Policy is available online at www.ReaderService.com or upon request from the Reader Service.

We make a portion of our mailing list available to reputable third parties that offer products we believe may interest you. If you prefer that we not exchange your name with third parties, or if you wish to clarify or modify your communication preferences, please visit us at www.ReaderService.com/consumerschoice or write to us at Reader Service Preference Service, P.O. Box 9062, Buffalo, NY 14269. Include your complete name and address.

KROM11B

ESSENCE BESTSELLING AUTHOR

GWYNNE FORSTER

A new story in the Harringtons series...

A U.S. ambassador, Scott Galloway's latest goal is to settle down and start a family. Yet Denise Miller, the one woman he can't stop thinking about, is also the one he ruled out years ago. Now their mutual friendship with the Harringtons has reunited them. With hearts this stubborn and passion this wild, can they find the compromise that leads to forever?

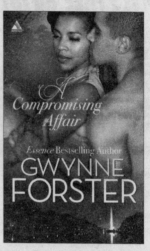

A COMPROMISING AFFAIR

"Forster's portrayal of endearing love, beautiful settings, warm-spirited characters, romantic interludes and mature and caring men makes this a delightful book romance lovers will enjoy."
—*RT Book Reviews* on *LOVE ME OR LEAVE ME*

Coming the first week of September 2011 wherever books are sold.

KIMANI PRESS™   www.kimanipress.com

KPGF4510911

ESSENCE BESTSELLING AUTHOR

DONNA HILL

An unhappy marriage taught Terri Powers never to trust again. Instead she put all her energy into creating the successful New York advertising agency she'd always dreamed of. Then she meets handsome, strong-willed businessman Clinton Steele. Try as she might, Terri can't fight the sensual attraction between them—or the desperate hunger that fires her deepest passions....

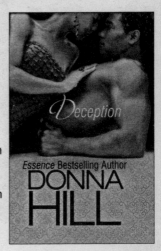

Deception

ESSENCE Bestselling Author
DONNA HILL

DECEPTION

"Once again, Donna Hill has created a novel of pure, unadulterated reading pleasure."
—*RT Book Reviews* on *DECEPTION*

Coming the first week of September 2011 wherever books are sold.

KIMANI PRESS™

www.kimanipress.com

KPDH4520911

Welcome to Chocolate Chateau—a top-secret resort where its A-list clientele explores their deepest sexual fantasies.

Kim Louise

ANYTIME

At Chocolate Chateau, the sultry "Dr. G." helps fulfill dreams. Gena Biven cherishes the business she's built, yet behind her sexy Dr. G persona, her own love life is in disarray—until she meets undercover reporter Marlowe Chambers. Their connection is explosive…but so are the secrets between them.

Kim Louise

ANYTIME

"Just the right amount of humor, passion and understanding. She keeps readers on edge from the beginning of the story through unexpected twists to a greatly satisfying conclusion."
—*RT Book Reviews* on *SWEET LIKE HONEY*

Coming the first week of September 2011 wherever books are sold.

KIMANI PRESS™

www.kimanipress.com

KPKL9950911